"I'm going to spoil you as much as I like, so just relax and enjoy it, okay?"

"Does anything look off to you?"

"You're adorable."

In the blink of an eye, threads of
shimmering gold fluttered past him,
and he felt something soft graze one
of his still-flushed cheeks.

©Hanekoto

Contents

Amane Fujimiya

A student who began living alone when he started high school. He's poor at every type of housework and lives a slovenly life. Has a low opinion of himself and tends to put himself down, but is kind at heart.

Mahiru Shiina

A classmate who lives in the apartment next door to Amane. The most beautiful girl in school; everyone calls her an "angel." Started cooking for Amane because she couldn't overlook his unhealthy lifestyle.

The Angel Next Door Spoils Me Rotten

4

Saekisan

ILLUSTRATION BY
Hanekoto

YEN ON

NEW YORK

The Angel Next Door Spoils Me Rotten 4

Saekisan

TRANSLATION BY NICOLE WILDER * COVER ART BY HANEKOTO

OTONARI NO TENSHISAMA NI ITSUNOMANIKA DAMENINGEN NI SARETEITA KEN Vol. 4
Copyright © 2021 Saekisan
Illustration © 2021 Hanekoto
All rights reserved.
Original Japanese edition published in 2021 by SB Creative Corp.
This English edition is published by arrangement with SB Creative Corp., Tokyo in care of Tuttle-Mori Agency, Inc., Tokyo.

English translation © 2022 by Yen Press, LLC

Yen On
150 West 30th Street, 19th Floor
New York, NY 10001

Visit us at yenpress.com * facebook.com/yenpress * twitter.com/yenpress
yenpress.tumblr.com * instagram.com/yenpress

First Yen On Edition: October 2022
Edited by Yen On Editorial: Shella Wu, Ivan Liang
Designed by Yen Press Design: Liz Parlett

Yen On is an imprint of Yen Press, LLC.
The Yen On name and logo are trademarks of Yen Press, LLC.

Library of Congress Cataloging-in-Publication Data
Names: Saekisan, author. | Hanekoto, illustrator. | Wilder, Nicole. translator.
Title: The angel next door spoils me rotten / Saekisan ; illustration by Hanekoto ; translation by Nicole Wilder.
Other titles: Otonari no tenshi-sama ni Itsu no ma ni ka dame ningen ni sareteita ken. English
Description: First Yen On edition. | New York : Yen On, 2020- |
Identifiers: LCCN 2020043583 | ISBN 9781975319236
(v. 1 ; trade paperback) |
ISBN 9781975322694 (v. 2 ; trade paperback) |
ISBN 9781975333409 (v. 3 ; trade paperback) |
ISBN 9781975344405 (v. 4 ; trade paperback)
Subjects: CYAC: Love—Fiction.
Classification: LCC PZ7.1.S2413 An 2020 | DDC [Fic]—dc23
LC record available at https://lccn.loc.gov/2020043583

ISBNs:978-1-9753-4440-5 (paperback)
978-1-9753-4441-2 (ebook)

1 2022

LSC-C

Printed in the United States of America

Chapter 1

The Angel's Thoughts

"We're not dating, but to me...he is the most important person on earth."

Mahiru had made that statement publicly, in front of their class-mates. For the rest of the day, Amane couldn't think about anything else or pay attention in class. He just didn't know exactly what she'd meant by "important." Did she mean that they were good friends, or affectionately close, or maybe—in a romantic sense?

The more he thought about it, the more anxiety and unease he felt, but the faintest hope swirled in his chest. All day, he was over-whelmed by emotions he could not put into words.

His friend Itsuki smiled at him, but didn't make any jokes or say anything about it.

Amane had little hope of figuring out what Mahiru was think-ing on his own. He spent the whole day irritated, wishing he could just ask her directly what she'd meant. But he never got the chance at school.

When the two of them got back to Amane's apartment, he finally, timidly, asked Mahiru.

She looked at him with a puzzled expression. "I wasn't lying, you know," she said without hesitation. It sounded like she had no idea why he was asking.

Mahiru put on her apron to prepare dinner. She also put on a little smile, perhaps aware of Amane's discomfort. "I'm fairly sociable, but my circle of friends is small. The only people I can definitely say I'm close with are you, Chitose, and Akazawa. Of course, all of you are important to me, but among the three of you, you're the one I'm closest with and the one I feel most at ease with when we're together."

"Oh, um..."

Amane knew that what Mahiru was saying was true, but being told this face-to-face felt very strange for some reason.

"We've spent the past half year or so together, and it has been a very meaningful time for me. I've never been the type to get close to others, and you're the most comfortable, most likable person I know," she said calmly and candidly.

Amane suppressed a groan as he looked into Mahiru's gentle eyes. She gazed back at him.

"For me, the world is a small place," she continued. "I could count the people I like on one hand, as if I'm living in a miniature garden... In my little world, you are the most precious person to me. You're the one who told me that I'm okay just the way I am."

"Mahiru..."

"So I want you to be a little more confident in that regard, Amane."

Mahiru's cheeks reddened, coloring her shy expression, clearly showing that she was stating her true feelings, but Mahiru didn't seem to notice.

The sincerity painted on her face caused conflicting emotions to well up inside Amane—embarrassment and indescribable joy threatened to make his chest burst.

"After all, you already know that I trust you above anyone else. Did you think that there was someone else that I liked?"

"That's not it, but…when you put it that way, you must have known how I would take it, right?"

"That's exactly right," Mahiru answered with an unwavering smile.

Amane stared at Mahiru. "So when you dodged the question that way, you knew it would open us up to insistent prying and suspicions of romance?"

Mahiru's smile broadened. She was oddly nonchalant. "That's also right."

"In that case, wouldn't it have been easier to manage the rumors by letting out a few snippets of information at a slow trickle? If people are going to speculate, I think it would be better to at least have some control over the direction the rumors take."

"…Indeed."

Amane knew that Mahiru had her own ways of thinking about these things, but to him, it had been extraordinarily nerve-racking to hear her talk about him in public, even indirectly.

In the end, there had been a big uproar after her statement, but Mahiru herself had just calmly put on her angelic smile. The boys in love with Mahiru were probably stressing out about it right now.

"Anyway, you should be more careful. If you don't say anything to me beforehand, I might get the wrong idea, too."

"Get the wrong idea?"

"…Usually, if someone said something like that about me, I'd think what everyone else is thinking."

Amane figured that Mahiru must like him in some way. Otherwise, she wouldn't be so relaxed around him, or look at him with such trust in her eyes. But he couldn't figure out the exact nature of her affection.

Was it the same kind of sentiment that Amane felt toward Mahiru, or was it something more passionate?

The feelings he held were not something that he could easily put into words.

He didn't feel burning-hot passion, and it wasn't intense, heart-rending yearning, either. It was more like a quiet, gentle candle giving off a steady heat. Mahiru was the first person for whom his heart had felt such affection and desire to treasure.

However, those weren't the kind of feelings that most friends of the opposite sex could just openly talk about. Also, Amane didn't know if Mahiru felt the same way. For this reason, he reminded himself to speak clearly, so as not to be misunderstood.

"I mean, if for example I were to announce that you were someone important to me, with that kind of timing, you'd start getting ideas too, right?"

"But I don't think you would ever make such a declaration in the first place, Amane."

"Well, that's true, but—"

"Or are you saying that's what you're going to do?"

"I know that if I did, I'd wind up feeling like I decided to sit down on a bed of thorns."

I know for sure that people's thorny gazes would skewer me—no, they'd eviscerate me. I would die by a thousand stares.

Amane waved his hand in front of his face. He had no intention of resigning himself to such a fate without any sort of preparation.

Mahiru let a little giggle slip out.

"I know you're not the risk-taking type."

"…Somehow, I feel like that annoys you."

"You're imagining things."

Amane was pretty sure he was not imagining the look of

exasperation on Mahiru's face, but it seemed she didn't feel like explaining anything to him.

Mahiru let out a deep sigh, as if to vent her frustrations, and headed for the kitchen.

"...Um?"

"What is it?"

"If I did make some kind of public declaration, I think it would have a big effect on your life, too... Are you prepared for that?"

"What a silly question. I would never suggest something if I wasn't ready to deal with the consequences."

Amane was at a loss for words because she really said it without a second thought. Mahiru didn't so much as look his way and started setting out her cooking utensils with a flourish of her apron hem.

"I understand that my social standing is different from yours, and that we receive very different kinds of attention. I also understand that you won't say anything. And I don't want to make you uncomfortable."

"...That's—"

"It's a real pain to be popular, you know. People are always watching how you act in public and meddling in your affairs."

Mahiru grumbled to herself, and it was plain to see she was fed up with the attention. Then she turned around to look at Amane.

"But here, it's just the two of us; there's no one to butt in. For now, I'm satisfied with that."

Mahiru smiled coyly, and Amane couldn't do anything but stare at her beautiful smile, unable to say anything more.

Chapter 2

The Angel's Risky Proposal

A new day had dawned since Mahiru's shocking statement, but the excitement over the angel's new relationship hadn't settled down at all in class.

Her words had attracted considerable curiosity, since up to now, she hadn't shown any interest in boys and had treated members of both sexes the same.

However, no matter what she was asked, Mahiru didn't answer with any additional information. Her closest friend, Chitose, also insisted that she didn't know anything, so whoever Mahiru had alluded to remained unknown.

As the boy in question, Amane was relieved by this, but at the same time, he was terrified, wondering when he would be exposed.

"Well, I think if someone got a reeeally good look at your face, they'd figure it out. But from a distance, just looking at your silhouette, I doubt anyone would recognize you," Itsuki said, laughing at Amane's concern as he looked over the merchandise for sale.

Amane had brought Itsuki and Yuuta along with him to the sports equipment store. He was there to buy some exercise gear, after deciding that he should start training and exercising to better complement

Mahiru, and so that she might fall for him. The impact of her statement had sparked the idea.

Club activities were suspended for the time being due to upcoming exams, so the track and field club ace had some free time and accompanied Amane to help him pick out running shoes.

"I mean, after all, you usually have a plain hairstyle and act all indifferent, so you come off as cold, and your expression doesn't really change," Itsuki said. "But when you're with her, you make all sorts of faces, and you actually look up from the ground, so you seem sweet and gentle. I don't think anyone would connect that guy with the Amane we see at school."

"You're pretty easy to read, Fujimiya; it's surprising," Yuuta added.

"Shut up."

Amane was aware that he acted more gently toward Mahiru than other people, but it was still embarrassing to hear someone point it out like that.

It was all the more humiliating to know that even Yuuta, who he had just started hanging out with, could see it.

Amane frowned, trying to shake off the embarrassment. Itsuki looked at him with a foolish grin.

"Looks like my prediction was right, that you would change when you found a girl you liked."

"…Shut up."

"Oooh, you are sooo cute when you're trying not to look embarrassed, Amane!"

"Don't be a creep, Itsuki."

"It is a little creepy, Itsuki."

"Why are you on his side, Yuuta? You're supposed to stick with me."

"Well, it's…you know."

"I'm gonna cry, guys."

Itsuki did not seem like he was going to cry at all. After grinning and poking at Amane for a while, he shrugged. "Well, I guess she really does have all sorts of troubles of her own, huh? Including yesterday's performance."

"...Performance? She told me she did it to control the rumors as best she could without telling any lies, since she was under suspicion anyway."

"Ah, is that how she explained it? Well, that's all true, but I think it was also an attempt to repel other guys without inviting hostility from other girls. When you're popular, you're always the object of jealousy, more or less. By hinting that she's got a special someone, and that she hasn't got eyes for anyone else, she's saying that even if she hangs around Yuuta and us once in a while, she's not interested."

"I see."

"Plus, you know, to keep it all in check."

"What do you mean?"

"...Ah, it's nothing. Forget it. Setting all that aside, I can see in your eyes that she's important to you, and I think she probably feels the same way. You can win her over if you push, or even better, push her down, heh? It's important for a guy to take a little initiative, you know!"

The words "push her down" made Amane recall the situation that happened over Golden Week.

I didn't mean to...

By accident, he had lost his balance and fallen on top of her. It wasn't anything intentional. There was no way he would have done it on purpose, being fully aware that Mahiru would hate him if he did something as outrageous as that.

However, if Mahiru made the same expression next time, looking like she was waiting for him to make some sort of move—he wasn't sure what he'd do then.

"…Hey, did something happen that I don't know about? Did you get lucky or something?"

Itsuki made a grabbing motion with his hands, very interested now that Amane's cheeks were gradually flushing with remembered shame.

"Just shut up for once!" Amane shouted.

"Itsuki, you're the worst!" Yuuta added.

"Whose side are you on, anyway?! I thought you were hoping for progress, Yuuta!"

"I don't want to be on your side when you're messing around like that. Though I do think that Fujimiya is being too passive."

"As far as I can tell, you're both against me."

Amane had complex feelings about getting these evaluations from Yuuta and Itsuki. On the other hand, he knew he wasn't particularly assertive, so he didn't feel like he could make much of a rebuttal.

"Now, now, we just wanted to give you a little nudge," Yuuta insisted. "I don't know Mahiru that well, so I'm just speculating, but I doubt she has feelings for anyone other than you, Fujimiya. It seems like you're the only one she really trusts. After all, she seems incredibly wary of most people. I'm telling you, the way that girl looks at you, and only you, is different."

"…I know that she trusts me, and that she likes me as a person, but even so…"

"Why are you so negative? Have some confidence. You're a good guy, and you seem like the kind of person who can put in some serious effort, so long as you have a goal. I mean, look, if you really don't have any confidence, then start working out and get in shape. Physical fitness is linked to emotional well-being, you know. If your body gets fitter, your attitude should improve, and if your attitude improves, everything around you will look brighter. By getting physically stronger, you can make yourself more confident."

"You sound awfully self-assured."

©Hanekoto

"I read it in a book."

Yuuta seemed amused at reciting something he saw in a book once and passing it off as if speaking from his own experience. He laughed playfully and clapped Amane on the shoulder. "Well, you're tall, Fujimiya, so you'd look good if you filled out a little, looked a little more balanced, you know? It would be a waste not to cultivate the good features you were born with."

"...I'll try my best."

"You've got Yuuta to help you with the physical part, and me for the emotional part," Itsuki said. "The dream team!"

"I'm a little apprehensive about your advice..."

"How rude!"

"Just kidding... I trust you, somewhat."

"This guy just can't be honest with his feelings."

Itsuki ribbed Amane with his elbow. Amane deliberately ignored his very existence and shifted his gaze back to Yuuta, who was smiling beside him.

Amane had already tried on and chosen some shoes, as well as the other things he needed. Figuring they would be in the way if they lingered too long in the store, he held up the merchandise in his hands to suggest that they hurry to the cashier.

"Kadowaki, should we go pay?"

"I guess you could. I thought I might get some new running wear, too."

"Isn't it a little cruel to ignore me, guys?"

Itsuki knew what they were up to, and shouted after them in a slightly disheartened voice as they headed for the registers. Amane and Yuuta looked at each other and laughed a little.

"...So what that means is, I'm going to do a little more exercise, so that will probably increase the amount of time I'm out of the house."

After getting home and devouring the entire dinner that Mahiru had made, Amane told her that he was going to be around the house less often.

Although his training would be something he did by himself, he figured that it would inconvenience her if he didn't say anything, since they spent a lot of time together and since she was in charge of fixing dinner.

Mahiru, who was relaxing comfortably on the sofa after dinner as usual, widened her caramel-colored eyes in slight surprise at Amane's words.

"I'll adjust the menu to account for exercise, but...this is quite sudden. Exercising is good, but what prompted this?"

"...I guess I just wanted to improve myself a little more, as a guy," Amane deflected.

Naturally, there was no way he could tell her openly that it was because he wanted her approval, or that he wanted to look as good as she did, or that he wanted her to find him attractive.

Mahiru's laughing rang like a clear and beautiful bell. "My goodness, that's a line I never thought I'd hear from the Amane who was living a slovenly life until half a year ago."

"Come on, don't make fun of me... There's no harm in focusing more on my studies, my fitness, or my appearance."

"Well, that's true, but..."

Amane let his eyes wander. Mahiru's gaze implied that she was surprised to hear something like this coming from him, but she didn't seem like she was going to question him any further.

Mahiru had an exasperated but somewhat charming smile, and she poked Amane's cheek with her fingertip teasingly.

"...Just don't overdo it, all right? You're an overachiever, Amane. I know that once you decide to do something, you follow through, so please ask someone for help if it looks like you might get carried away."

"I'm not worried about that. I've got a trainer."

"Kadowaki?"

"He's not an actual instructor, but he can teach me all sorts of basic things."

"I guess that makes me your personal chef. I'll think carefully about nutritional balance when I make your meals."

If Amane was going to start exercising and getting in shape, then naturally he would need to change his diet, too. Since he was already skinny, he knew he needed to put on some weight, which meant eating more in general. That in turn meant more work for Mahiru.

Amane knew he depended on Mahiru for most of his meals, so he felt bad about asking even more from her, but she accepted the challenge without so much as a sour look.

"Sorry for causing you all sorts of trouble."

"No, if you've made up your mind, I'll be glad to help and cheer you on, but...you mustn't forget that first we have exams to get through, all right?"

"I haven't forgotten. I've been reviewing every day."

"That's great."

Amane couldn't summon the willpower to shake her off as she patted his head and praised him in a soft voice that oozed sweetness.

But he also had mixed feelings about not putting up any resistance, so he shot her a slightly reproachful look.

"...Don't make fun of me. I'm perfectly capable of balancing my studies with my training."

Amane was earnest by nature and took his classes seriously. He was the type who could mostly grasp the material just by sitting through the lesson. Since he also never failed to review and prepare at home, he basically had no worries when it came to academics.

He wouldn't be neglecting his studies just by diverting a little of that energy to exercise. In fact, he intended to get more serious about his studies as well. He was determined not to fall behind in either department, lest he fail to keep up with Mahiru.

"You'll tire yourself out doing that. Shall I pamper you once for good luck?"

"Look here—"

"Well, should you ever request it, I'll pamper you any time, so—" Mahiru patted her chest reassuringly and smiled.

The memory of burying his face in the soft flesh there the other day made Amane press his lips together.

Mahiru had only embraced him in an attempt to console him when he seemed down, but it was the sort of gesture that had particular significance to a boy of his age. At the time, he had been so caught up in his emotions that he had been more preoccupied with the kindness she had shown him than the physical sensations of the embrace.

Next time, Amane knew he would take in and savor the feeling of her body. Precisely because he was aware of how shameless that would be, he wanted to refrain.

"…It's frightening how you seem willing to do anything I ask," he muttered.

"I mean, if it's something I'm able to do, I'll do what I can. Of course, I expect to be repaid, though."

"I think I would feel even worse if you did all sorts of things for me without any expectation of repayment."

"But when it comes to acts of selfless love and altruism, in most cases, a sense of emotional satisfaction is pretty much the only compensation, right?"

"Incidentally, how do you want me to thank you?"

"…I'd like you to listen to a request of mine."

This was Mahiru, so Amane wasn't expecting her to ask for money or anything, but he snickered unintentionally at the sweet way she asked for such vague restitution.

"Sure, as long as it's something I'm able to do. Any kind of fair exchange."

"My request is pretty selfish."

"Somehow I doubt that."

"It really is... You can only say that because you don't know the true extent of my selfishness."

"All right, let's hear it, then. What's your request?" Amane figured that if she was making such a big deal about it, it must be something major. He was curious to know what a big request from Mahiru might be.

Mahiru's face stiffened slightly.

When Amane stared directly into her pretty caramel-colored eyes, wondering what on earth she was about to say, she started to let her gaze wander.

Amane couldn't make out whether Mahiru's wish was truly something so significant that she was hesitant to say it out loud, or if she was just putting on an act.

He stared intently at her as her cheeks gradually reddened.

"Well..."

"Yes?"

"Umm, it's..."

"It's...?"

"...A-Amane, I want you to pat my head, too."

Without meaning to, Amane smiled stiffly at Mahiru, who had started to say something else, and helplessly made that desperate plea in her panic to avoid voicing her original request.

"Is that what you're going with? There was something else you were about to say, wasn't there?"

"It's fine."

He was curious to know what she had been about to say, but

thought it would put her in a bad mood if he pressed anymore, so he left it there and extended a hand.

He did pat her head occasionally, but it was rare for Mahiru herself to ask for it. He would do this sort of thing anytime she asked without expecting anything in return, and in fact, he very much enjoyed it, so long as Mahiru didn't hate it. But he did find it adorable that she had humbly asked for it out loud.

The tension visibly left Mahiru's face as Amane stroked her head just as she had requested.

"I don't know what part of this is supposed to be selfish, though."

"It *is* selfish. Because I want you to touch me more."

"Touch you?"

Amane's movements stiffened. Before he noticed her moving, Mahiru was looking up at him with her usual soft face and glistening eyes.

"I like it when you touch me, Amane. I don't usually enjoy making physical contact with people, but I think your hands feel nice."

"Is that…so?"

Mahiru seemed oblivious to the implications of what she'd just said. She was wearing her usual gentle expression as she nudged closer to him, pleadingly.

As the distance between them narrowed, Amane could smell her sweet scent more clearly, and his heartbeat inevitably quickened.

…I think this girl might be trying to kill me.

Any normal guy would count himself lucky to hear the girl he liked say that she wanted him to touch her; he'd probably go ahead and do it, knowing what he was getting into.

Amane was a healthy young man, and the invitation was very tempting, but he also knew that Mahiru was so affectionate with him because of how deeply she trusted him.

"You don't touch me often, Amane, but when you do, you do it in a way that's gentle and thoughtful, don't you? It's really calming, and it feels nice. I think you emit a soothing aura or something."

Mahiru was probably teasing Amane, at least a little.

"...It's not all that relaxing for me, you know. You're a girl, Mahiru, so it's not like I can touch you thoughtlessly."

"I don't mind."

"I do. Let me try telling you to touch me; I bet you'll feel uncomfortable."

He cautioned against it a little too strongly—deep down, he was still feeling insecure about the fact that she didn't seem to think of him as a real man.

In response, he got a placid smile and the question, "...Will you touch me?"

It felt like she was carelessly trying to provoke him. Against his better judgment, he pinched Mahiru's squishy cheeks. In a sense, he did touch her as asked, but the dissatisfaction on Mahiru's face was evident.

"Come on, I won't mention it outside this apartment, and I won't ask the same of anyone but you, Amane..."

"Absolutely not, don't be ridiculous."

Amane didn't mean it that way, but his answer came out almost in a growl, filled with emotion. He was flustered, hearing words that she would only say to him.

Amane was frantically trying to get ahold of himself and all the unspeakable thoughts that were filling his mind. He cupped Mahiru's hands in his. That was as much touching as he could allow himself.

Mahiru blinked, fluttering her long eyelashes, and gave Amane a gentle smile that looked just a little embarrassed. He could clearly see relief and happiness in her expression, which made him feel embarrassed, too.

"…You feel warm. Speaking of, sometimes you get really warm."

"…I'll let go this instant."

"No, don't. As I expected, your hands are warm, and big, and rugged…very different from mine."

"You're small, and dainty, and delicate, so I feel anxious touching you."

"I won't break that easily. Besides, when you touch me, you're always gentle. I can tell right away that you would absolutely never hurt me."

"…I'd never be rough with any girl."

Amane was absolutely sure that he would never knowingly hurt the girl he wanted to cherish forever. To him, she was someone very delicate who he wanted to protect from harm.

Even though he knew she wasn't fragile, he carefully stroked the back of Mahiru's hand as if he was touching a fragile piece of porcelain, and she narrowed her caramel-colored eyes as if it tickled.

"…That's exactly why I trust you and why I'm asking you to touch me." Mahiru smiled.

She was overwhelmingly lovely, and, suppressing the urge to embrace her right then and there and make her his, Amane mirrored her smile.

Chapter 3

The Angel in the Dream, Feelings of Shame

"...I love you."

A voice full of anticipation spoke these few, simple words.

Her voice was quiet as it left her soft, pink lips, and she approached him seductively.

Amane was propping himself up on the bed, and she lowered her hips onto his legs, pinning him in place.

Strangely, he didn't feel any weight at all.

But the soft touch of her skin and her fragrant smell filled his senses.

Mahiru leaned coquettishly up against him and wrapped her arms around his back, closing the gap between them as she cast her eyes down shyly. Amane looked down and saw a fresh expanse of skin that normally never saw the light of day, peeking from the neckline of her white dress.

He tried to avert his gaze from the deep valley between her breasts, but Mahiru moved her hands from his back up to his neck and pulled his face closer, as if to tell him not to look away.

A sigh escaped her lips.

"...Touch me more?" she whispered.

©Hanekoto

Amane wrapped his arms around her delicate back and slowly brought his lips closer—

"—Ah?"

He sat up straight.

Amane was alone in his bedroom. The morning sun shone into the room through a gap in the closed curtains.

When he looked at the clock on his side table, he saw that it was just past five.

With the approach of summer, the sun was rising earlier—it was early enough to get a start on the day, although Amane certainly hadn't intended to wake up at this hour.

He pressed the palm of his hand against his face as he remembered what he'd been dreaming about and was immediately overcome with shame.

This is the worst...

The dream had taken him by surprise.

Previously, when Mahiru had appeared in his dreams, she had behaved as usual—never acting with such blatant desire. When she'd told him the day before that she wanted him to touch her more, that must have provided the inspiration for his fantasy, but even so, he felt ashamed. His mind had imagined Mahiru acting in ways she never would. Even though it had only been a dream, he still felt guilty about having those kinds of feelings toward her.

It was very frustrating—he wanted to cherish Mahiru and treat her respectfully, but his subconscious mind apparently had other ideas. He had the fleeting temptation to slam his head into the wall.

Amane decided that some exercise would be just the thing to clear his head. Pushing away his subconscious desires, he made to leave his room, but paused on the way out.

"...Kill me now."

Before he could start the day, he was going to need a nice long shower to wash away any lingering frustrations.

"Hey, Amane, what's with the dead expression?"

After getting up, Amane had gone for an early morning run to shake off his shame, exhausting himself both physically and mentally. Chitose must have noticed, and approached him during a break at school.

Amane looked at Itsuki, who was sitting beside him, to ask whether he looked that lifeless, and Itsuki nodded.

"Ah, well...I went for a little run this morning," Amane explained.

"That'll wipe you out, no doubt." Chitose nodded. "A couch potato is sure to get groggy when they finally start working out." Chitose cackled and grinned lightheartedly as she slapped him on the back.

Amane was relieved that she didn't press him any further.

Telling Chitose something meant that Mahiru would know eventually anyway, so Amane did his best to avoid telling her anything important. Honestly, he didn't want to let anyone know about his dream.

"If you're not feeling well, you ought to go right home after school's over and rest. It's best not to overdo it," Mahiru added, standing beside Chitose like her chaperone.

They were at school, so Mahiru was in her "angel mode," but her concern was genuine. Amane had a feeling she was going to spoil him when they got home.

However, Amane knew that he wouldn't be able to accept her kindness—his lingering guilt over the dream wouldn't even allow him to look Mahiru in the eye.

Without meeting her gaze, Amane responded flatly, "Thank you for your concern. I'm fine, so there's no need to worry." He did his best not to allow any emotion to creep into his words. From the corner of his eye, he could see Mahiru's expression stiffen slightly.

Amane was trying not to let the awkwardness he felt every time he looked at Mahiru show on his face, but from her perspective, it probably seemed like he had suddenly gotten angry at her.

He couldn't possibly explain the reason for his icy demeanor, so there was nothing to do but keep his mouth shut and evade the issue.

Everyone knew that Amane was a gloomy introvert, downright unsociable really, so nothing about this behavior should have aroused anyone's suspicions.

"...Are you feeling unwell, Amane?" Mahiru asked.

"No, I'm not sick, I'm just tired," he replied. "Really, I'm trying my best to not fall asleep. We've got tests coming up, so I can't very well sleep through class now."

"Geez! So serious." Chitose giggled.

"You should try to be more serious, too," he chided. "Our school's exams are hard, so stop playing around and try studying for a change."

"Speaking of exams, I think it would be more fun, and more effective, if we did our studying all together, don't you?" Chitose asked.

"Oh? Then perhaps Shiina ought to tutor you."

"I guess that would work, but..."

Chitose was staring hard at Amane, but he refused to make eye contact with her. He pulled the materials for the next class out of his desk and directed his attention toward arranging them.

If he participated any longer in the conversation, he would inevitably have to talk to Mahiru. He sighed softly and leafed through a textbook as if the rest of the discussion was no concern of his.

Amane left school promptly after classes ended, did the evening's shopping, and returned home.

As usual, Mahiru was already in his apartment, preparing food, but she was obviously feeling dejected.

She seemed to be able to sense that something was different about his mood and kept glancing over at him and frowning. Often at home, they would act a little more familiar, but that evening, she carefully maintained a sense of distance that was not all that different from how she behaved at school.

Amane still felt terribly awkward, and he tried to push thoughts of Mahiru out of his mind as best he could. It was easy to understand how she might interpret that as him ignoring her.

"Are you mad at me...?" Mahiru asked nervously, after they had finished eating dinner without even looking at each other once.

Realizing his error, Amane looked up at her.

Mahiru's eyes flickered with anxiety.

"I'm not mad," he replied.

"People only answer that way when they're mad. You've been acting strange all day, and you're being terse with me... Did I do something to upset you without realizing it...?"

Even though Amane had clearly been the one avoiding her, Mahiru sounded apologetic, which made him realize that he had only been thinking about his own personal discomfort.

Flustered, Amane took Mahiru's hands in his and peered into her eyes, which were more tearful than usual.

"N-no, that's not it. You didn't do anything, Mahiru. I'm sorry for hurting your feelings."

"So then, why...why are you acting so cold?"

"W-well, um, there are a number of reasons, I guess you could say..."

Amane found himself faltering when it came time to offer any.

He obviously knew he couldn't be too honest—a girl like Mahiru would definitely be put off by something like that. He didn't want to put her in an awkward position or make her uncomfortable around him later.

"I've been wondering if maybe you'd gotten tired of me or something…"

"Absolutely not!" Amane insisted. "I-I've just got some personal stuff going on… There's just a lot on my mind."

"…And you're not going to tell me about it?"

Mahiru frowned dejectedly and looked at the floor. Amane could only groan.

How can I possibly explain?

He hated lying to her, so he decided the best course of action was to only tell her the mildest version of the truth. Though he wasn't sure exactly how to round off the rough edges or sound vague in this particular case.

If he messed up, she wouldn't understand, and she might even be repulsed instead.

"It—it's no big deal, really, okay?"

"…Even though it's something bad enough to make you ignore me?"

"No, the thing is, I mean, how do I put this? I'm doing it to exercise self-control, or, like, to settle my mind down."

"You don't feel calm when I'm around?"

"That's not what I mean, it's just, it's d-difficult."

"So it's hard to spend time with me?"

"That's not what I said! Geez, how can I say this…?"

If she was a boy, it would have been easy. Amane wasn't sure he could put it in a way that a girl would understand, no matter what he said to her. Yet he had to tell her something, or she would misunderstand again.

Mahiru obviously wanted to know why he was avoiding her if she hadn't done anything wrong, but all Amane could manage to tell her was that it was hard to explain.

For the sake of his likely nonexistent pride, he needed to put it as delicately as possible.

"...So you said that you want me to touch you more," he explained tentatively. "And because of that, how do I say this, I...had a, uh, a dream."

"A...dream?"

"...A dream where you were pleading with me, very sweetly, for certain things..."

Somehow, that was the best answer Amane could come up with.

Mahiru made a face like she didn't understand what he was talking about. She blinked her wide eyes dramatically.

"R-really, I hate that I dreamed something like that," Amane continued. "I try to avoid seeing you that way, and I would never be pushy about touching you. But this time I just...it's because yesterday, you...you were saying such cute things. And then, about me avoiding you awkwardly...it wasn't because I was mad at you or anything, it was because I was disgusted with myself..."

"...How exactly was I pleading with you, Amane?"

"Are you trying to embarrass me?!" he balked. Mahiru hadn't recoiled from him, which was good, but her curiosity seemed somehow even more dangerous, and he could feel his face twitching.

Dreams supposedly reflected desires, so if he told her what he had dreamed, she would then know he thought of her and looked at her in that way, even if it was not on purpose.

"Embarrass you...? No, I was just thinking I must have been really aggressive, if it was enough to make you feel uncomfortable. So I wanted to know, for reference."

"You don't need to know. What sort of reference would that be useful for anyway?"

"...Like for when I'm trying to make your heart race."

"Would you please stop trying to give me a heart attack?"

Amane didn't understand why Mahiru seemed to enjoy torment-
ing him. She had already found plenty of questionable ways to surprise him, so he didn't want to give her any more ideas.

Mahiru looked relieved, like she'd completely forgotten about
any concern or anxiety that had been previously troubling her. Her
cheeks had reddened faintly, probably because Amane had let the
word "cute" slip out of his mouth.

"It's a relief to hear that I'm not being shunned—I'm glad we
cleared that up."

For some reason, Mahiru's mouth curled upward in a good-
humored smile. She stared contently at Amane, who had his own lips
tightly drawn in shame and embarrassment.

"Amane, you're kind of…well, among the boys I know, you're the
most innocent."

"Oh, be quiet, I could say the same about you."

"I'm sure you would have been more surprised if you'd learned
that I was used to being in the company of males quite often… Really,
though, I've never spent much time around boys before. You're the
only one I'm this close with, Amane."

"…A-and I hardly ever associate with girls, so…"

Amane was aware that he sounded pathetic, but he couldn't bring
himself to lie. Anyway, if he had tried to pass himself off as someone who spent a lot of time with girls, Mahiru probably would have
laughed at him.

"Well, you seem pretty good at handling girls, all things considered," she remarked.

"You must be joking," Amane scoffed. "I can't handle anything.
I'm just…I always try to do what's right, and be decent, like my parents always said. And if I do anything bad, I try to balance it out by
doing something to make you happy, that's all. I'm happy when you're
happy…surely there's nothing wrong with that?"

"Nothing at all." Mahiru nodded. "You're sly that way, Amane."

"What's that supposed to mean?"

"Everything about you is sly."

"Are you trying to put me down…?"

"No, it's the opposite. I'm trying my best to encourage you, to get you to have more self-confidence."

"…I don't understand what you're getting at, though."

"That's fine, you don't have to understand right now."

This wasn't the first time they'd had this exchange, and Amane still didn't know what about him was supposed to be devious.

But Amane didn't think he needed to try too hard to find the answer.

Mahiru had been so concerned and dejected by Amane's behavior. Now, though, she was smiling cheerfully without the least bit of worry.

"Anyway, I got to hear something good today," she said.

"Something good?"

"You said that I'm the first person of the opposite sex you've ever been this close with."

Amane responded to Mahiru's outrageous statement with a sudden coughing fit.

Mahiru looked up at him curiously. It didn't seem like she had intended to provoke a reaction from him. She had probably just said what was on her mind. That was what made it so shocking for Amane.

"Th-that's misleading… Well, it's not misleading, but you make it sound weird! And it's none of your business anyway!" he stammered.

"Why are you getting so flustered? It's kind of nice, isn't it? Since I'm having all these firsts, too. It means that we've both fumbled our way closer together, right?"

"…Well, that's true, but…"

Thinking about how things had been up to this point, her observation did seem reasonable, but it felt overwhelmingly embarrassing to hear her say it so purely, without any other intentions. The more he tried not to overthink it, the more it weighed on him.

"...Amane?"

"It's nothing, so don't look at me, please."

He didn't want her to see the shame that was practically oozing off of him again, and he turned his back to her without rising from the sofa.

He didn't want to be seen, and he didn't want to look at her, either.

"Why are you speaking so stiffly?"

"Don't worry about it."

"...All right, I won't look."

Instead, Mahiru turned and sat with her back to his, so that she was able to lean against him. He turned his head to look at her and got a jab in the ribs.

He couldn't see her face, but he was certain she was grinning mischievously.

"If we sit like this, I'm 'not looking,' right?"

"...I guess not."

"Well, you'll just have to deal with it, since I had to deal with you avoiding me all day."

When she put it that way, Amane could tell that there was no way he was going to pull himself out of the hole he'd dug, and he wasn't even going to bother trying.

Feeling a strange sort of tranquility, though the warmth gradually spreading through his back was making his chest throb, Amane let his chin rest on his knees.

"...Please don't tell people about your first time or whatever anymore," he mumbled. "I really don't know how to endure it."

He felt Mahiru shiver, as if she had only just then remembered the issue. Then, apparently, she turned around, because he felt her grab the back of his shirt.

"Th-that's not what I meant to say at all, okay?! Well, it is, but I didn't say it with *that* in mind!"

"I—I understand, so just don't say any more."

Knowing that Mahiru had never been so close to anyone made it even more embarrassing when she talked about things like that.

It didn't take much thought to realize that the two of them had experienced a lot of firsts together.

At least in Amane's case, Mahiru was the first girl he had held hands with, except for his mother when he was a young child. Mahiru was also the only one he had ever embraced. It was very likely the same for her.

To get to be part of these new experiences with the girl he liked, to be the first step for her, was delightful, embarrassing, and an honor.

Amane found himself wishing that he could be her first and last love as well.

He smiled quietly to himself as Mahiru put her forehead against his back and rubbed against him out of embarrassment. How nice it would be to stay by her side in the future, he thought.

Chapter 4

Studying with the Angel

Things between Amane and Mahiru seemed to be back to normal the following day, and Chitose and Itsuki appeared relieved—apparently, they had been quite concerned. Amane's behavior had only changed slightly, but it must have been enough for them to notice.

The events of the previous day weighed heavily on Amane's mind, but he wasn't acting as awkwardly with Mahiru anymore. There were still some things that were bothering him, but as long as they were in school, he couldn't say a word about them.

Mahiru was giving everyone her usual angelic smile. She was currently surrounded by female classmates pestering her to teach them how to study.

Midterms were starting next week, and the girls must have wanted Mahiru, the top genius in the grade, to be their tutor. There was a touch of bewilderment mixed into Mahiru's gentle smile.

"I don't mind helping you all prepare for the tests, but I might not have enough room to host everyone..."

Thinking this wasn't going to be good, Amane pricked up his ears to listen in. It seemed that the girls who wanted to study with Mahiru y could do it at her place. They were probably curious to see what her apartment was like.

That would be a problem, since Mahiru is such a private person.

Although they weren't strangers, they weren't exactly friends, either, not like Chitose was. It would be very difficult for Mahiru to let them into her home.

From Amane's perspective, too, he didn't want them coming around where he lived if it could be avoided, just in case they caught wind of anything. He could just imagine the girls prying into every detail, while he endured resentment from the boys.

"Ah, no fair, no fair! I want help, too!"

"Me toooo!"

Then, other girls who had overheard the conversation put their hands up as well, and Mahiru was understandably wearing a troubled expression. Clearly there was no way so many people could fit in her apartment.

To make matters worse, the boys were looking over enviously.

"...Um, we could study together for an hour or two in the classroom after school today," Mahiru suggested, as a compromise. Their classroom had plenty of space. Despite that, there didn't seem to be an end to the chorus of voices asking to join. Club activities were paused during exams, so it was probably much easier for people to gather than usual.

As he listened to the loud shouts of his classmates from across the room, Amane couldn't help but feel bad for Mahiru.

With a strangely cheerful grin, Itsuki prodded Amane. "You're not going to take part?"

"Would there be any point?" he replied. "I already know everything that's going to be on the tests, and even if I didn't, with so many people, there won't be much time for everyone's questions anyway. Trust me, I'm better off studying on my own."

"Well, I certainly must commend your discipline, Amane, but I think we'd better join this study session anyway. It's a matter of motivation."

"I've always liked studying, so my motivation has always been—"

"Not yours, hers."

Amane looked over at Mahiru, making plans for a study session with more than half the class. It was obvious that she was going to have a hard time with so many people. She would probably feel better with a friend in the room. Finally, it began to dawn on Amane that he ought to attend, whether or not he felt the need to.

"...Even though there's not really anything for her to teach me?" he asked.

"It'll be fine," Itsuki insisted. "Look, you can tutor me. See, Chitose is going to join in, so I was gonna be stuck waiting for her anyway. There's no harm in studying a little while I'm there, eh?"

"Teaching other people is not my strong point..."

"Well, sure, the way you talk is can be a bit unfriendly, and you're not exactly the type to patiently explain things...but you wouldn't just let me fail, right?"

Amane faltered in the face of Itsuki's confident voice and gaze.

"I'm countin' on you, pal!" Itsuki cackled and clapped Amane on the shoulder.

Amane gave up on turning him down and just nodded.

Usually, after class ended, a handful of students might hang around for a while. But that day, there was a bustle of activity that was truly rare to see.

The desks, which had been neatly arranged during cleaning time, were now pushed together to form several clusters, and students assembled themselves with their groups of friends. Even the boys from class joined, which meant there were six times as many people as there should have been.

Amane sat facing Itsuki in the seat farthest away from Mahiru.

"...I can't be very much help like this, can I?" he whispered.

"I'm ready to learn, teacher!" Itsuki replied.

"...Wouldn't we be better off at home?"

"I'm just here to study while I wait for Chi. Besides, *she's* going to be late getting home, and you wouldn't want to leave her on her own, right?"

Amane narrowed his eyes at Itsuki, who was giving him a pointed look, but Itsuki just laughed.

Mahiru usually tried to get home before dark if she could, but because of the study session, she was sure to be late. Mahiru was a very cautious person and even carried a personal safety alarm around with her, but Itsuki was right, it probably wouldn't be good to let her go back alone in the dark.

On the other hand, Amane couldn't possibly walk her home with all their classmates watching, so he would have to keep his distance and stealthily watch over her as they walked.

"You don't seem to see this for the opportunity it is, Amane..."

"What, you want me to turn into some sort of predator now? That's not me, and personally, I have a problem with the idea of taking advantage of someone's carelessness to make a move."

"That attitude of yours must be how you've gained her trust. Well, you guys will be heading back to the same place, so I guess there's no point trying anything on the way anyhow. It's not like you won't have plenty of chances to make your move."

"It's not like I would anyway! If I made her hate me, or made her cry, I'd die."

Mahiru left him plenty of openings, since she let him inside her defenses. Even so, Amane had never considered seizing one of those chances to try anything. Rather, he had always warned her about letting her guard down.

If he tried anything with Mahiru when she was being careless because of her trust in him, their happy relationship could very well disappear. Amane didn't want to lose her trust, or his dignity.

Itsuki knew what his friend was like. He shrugged in a slightly exasperated manner, but Amane paid him no attention and opened his textbook to the material that would be covered on the exams.

"Look, I'm all good here, so why don't you tell me where we should start? I don't have trouble with anything, which means it's up to you to point out the sections you don't understand if you want to get anything done." Amane drummed his fingers on the pages and pressed his friend for an answer.

"Dodging the issue, huh?" Itsuki grinned and opened his own book.

Itsuki wasn't stupid or anything—in fact, he was quite capable. He had a good understanding of his own abilities and was the type who could produce good results with minimal effort. He just found studying a bore and goofed off a lot to annoy his parents. Fundamentally, he had an earnest disposition.

Amane had heard that in middle school, Itsuki had been an honors student, but when he'd started hanging out with Chitose, it apparently caused some trouble at home and kicked off his rebellious phase.

"I seriously do not understand English sentences," Itsuki complained.

"Maybe you should start by memorizing the vocabulary... For now, you can begin with the words and sentences that are sure to show up on the test. You slept through the class when the teacher went over the exam material, but he did tell us what to expect." Itsuki rarely skipped class, but he often fell asleep. Amane poked him in the forehead and continued.

"For the time being, I'll make another copy of my notes for you. There's a limit to how much you can cram for the long reading comprehension section. Basically, at this point, it's probably impossible to learn it all. Don't worry about doing it perfectly, but just try not to miss the vocabulary and multiple-choice questions. As long as you know at least a little bit, on most multiple-choice questions you can narrow it down to two answers, so we should work on getting you to where you can reliably pick the correct one out of the two. Let's place the most emphasis on scoring attainable points. You're just barely passing English, right?"

"Whew, you're a lifesaver, man! I'll thank you later by giving you a push in the right direction."

"I do *not* need you to do that. It's none of your concern."

Amane wanted to progress slowly in his relationship with Mahiru, in his own way, so if Itsuki pushed him too hard, he was liable to resist out of spite.

Itsuki met his friend's refusal with a frustrated look, but Amane wasn't inclined to change his opinion.

Before he could worry about progressing in their relationship, Amane wanted to improve himself enough that he would feel confident about being with Mahiru. To do that, he needed to prioritize his studies.

Itsuki seemed like he was about to say something else, but Amane ignored him, and once he had counted the number of pages in the notebook he was going to copy, he slammed it shut. "Good grief," Amane said as he picked up his mechanical pencil.

Itsuki assumed a studying posture, and with quiet relief, Amane glanced over in Mahiru's direction.

Just like always, she was smiling as she kindly explained the material to her classmates. As he watched her circulate busily through the room, smiling at everyone equally, Amane thought to himself that being the campus angel must be a tough role to play.

"Why can't I get the answer here?"

"Use the formula."

"I'm using it, but I'm not getting the answer!"

Chitose's group was studying together while chatting happily, and their cluster of desks was especially lively. However, a different group of boys seemed to be in trouble.

Even Mahiru wasn't able to follow up with every single person, and depending on each individual's ability to comprehend the material, it could take time to teach them. On top of that, Mahiru kept getting called over by the rowdiest students, so even though she was trying to help those classmates who weren't incessantly demanding her attention, she couldn't avoid getting pulled this way and that.

Amane hesitated for a moment over what to do, then stood up from his seat.

He walked over to the classmates who were frowning in frustration and looked over their shoulders to check the part in the text and the equation that was tripping them up. Then he slowly pointed to the relevant section in the textbook.

His classmates looked up at him, seemingly surprised by his sudden appearance, but Amane turned a blind eye to their stares and walked them through the problem.

In this group's case, they were simply using the wrong formula to solve the question, so it was easy to sort things out once Amane pointed out the issue that was giving them trouble.

Amane felt relieved that they had accepted his help despite his abrupt intrusion. He made eye contact with the boy sitting across from him, who was blinking repeatedly.

"I'm not Shiina, but it looks like she has her hands full. Sorry for butting in."

"...No, I'm grateful for the help," the boy said. "But I didn't expect you to come over and say something, Fujimiya."

"Well, you looked like you were having trouble," Amane responded.

He found it almost darkly comical just how cold and unfriendly everyone always assumed he was, but he knew it was true that he could be unsociable and downright gloomy, so he couldn't deny it.

Amane was turning to leave with an awkward smile when the classmate across from him asked, "So what about this one?" and showed Amane another problem he couldn't work out.

Since he was there already, Amane demonstrated how to solve that question, too.

The other boys all looked at each other, then for some reason, over at Itsuki.

"Hey, Itsuki! Can we borrow Fujimiya?"

"Well, he's mine, but I guess there's no helping it." Itsuki grinned.

"Since when did I become yours?"

Amane feigned offense at Itsuki's comment. He noticed that his friend was cheerfully pushing their two desks over to the boys in the study group. Amane was shocked at how quickly Itsuki joined them.

He didn't really mind, but he wished Itsuki had asked his permission first.

Amane sighed and sat back down in his own seat, which had been integrated into the new group. As he did, he kicked Itsuki lightly below the desks.

"Just so you know, I'm not that good at teaching," he stated.

"Well, thanks even so," one of the boys said. "Miss Angel looks busy over there."

"We all joined in at the last minute," another added, "so Shiina can't make it around to everyone on her own."

They were staring longingly at the group that Mahiru was tutoring, but it wasn't exactly envy in their eyes. They simply looked disappointed.

"We decided to come because it sounded fun, figuring we'd be lucky to receive any help, so getting help from Fujimiya is fine with us."

"Well, ideally the angel, 'cause she's cute and I'd be happier, but…"

"Well, don't expect me to be cute," Amane said, smiling wryly. "So show me the part you don't understand…?"

Amane prided himself on not having an ounce of cuteness to him. As a fellow guy, though, he understood what the others were trying to say. Who wouldn't prefer to be tutored by a friendly and intelligent girl like Mahiru, rather than an unsociable guy like him? Anybody would have been happier with her.

Amane shrugged, then asked them where they needed help and explained the material to them.

Fortunately, Amane was able to explain all the problems, and since the other students had asked for his help, they tackled the material earnestly and came to understand it fairly quickly.

Even Itsuki joined in with the other four students, asking questions and solving example problems. It was hard enough for Amane to handle four additional people, so things must have been even more difficult for Mahiru.

With that thought, Amane looked over in her direction and saw her answering questions for the neighboring group.

However, none of the questions were related to the exam material.

"…Do I have a type?"

Mahiru pondered the question curiously as the girls who had asked looked at her with keen interest.

The girls seemed to have changed tactics on Mahiru, who had been stubbornly refusing to reveal anything about the boy she had mentioned. Now they were trying to gather information indirectly on what kind of person he might be. Mahiru had never stated outright whether the mystery boy was her boyfriend or someone she liked, but even so, as one might expect, they all seemed to assume that she was interested in him.

The girls hadn't asked their question very loudly, but the surrounding groups still overheard it, and all the students in the classroom strained their ears for the answer, even as they continued working on their own practice problems.

"Let me think...," Mahiru said. "In terms of absolute requirements, I suppose he would have to be a kind and honest person. I don't like dishonest people at all."

"And what about appearance?"

"I think what's inside is more important, so I'm not too particular about looks," Mahiru replied. "...But someone who keeps themselves tidy would be good."

The answer that she gave, with a tender smile and look in her eye, was more about the kind of person she preferred than the kind of boy she liked, giving the impression that she was evading the question.

The girls who had asked the question must have also felt that she was being vague, and they stared at Mahiru with a hint of disappointment on their faces. Mahiru smiled back at them as always, but this time, it was tinged with bitterness.

"When I think about what else might be important, I guess... someone whose values match mine?"

"Values? Not hobbies and stuff?"

"Yes, values." Mahiru nodded. "I doubt they will ever match up perfectly, so I'm not expecting that, but I think it's important that we respect each other's values, even if they don't align. Someone who would never force their point of view, or try to change their partner... Yes, someone who appreciates their partner's ideas would be good. It would probably be best if it was someone who saw things the same way, but I like people who stand by their partner and accept their beliefs, even if they can't."

Mahiru brought her speech to a finish with a gentle smile, and her gaze darted over to Amane for just a second.

He reflexively averted his eyes, and Mahiru returned her focus to the group of girls with no change in her expression.

Amane knew that the people around him would start to notice if he stared at Mahiru any longer, so he lowered his gaze to the note-book in his hands. But then he heard a quiet chuckle from beside him, from someone who had been watching his behavior.

"And that's that, ladies and gentlemen."

Itsuki had observed while everyone else had abruptly stopped working. The boys Itsuki and Amane were studying with seemed to realize what was going on, and they quickly went back to their own notebooks in an attempt to feign ignorance.

Amane was turning pages and applying sticky notes as if nothing had happened, as he mulled over the idea of matching values.

Mahiru was the type of person who could never date anyone casually, and if she was with someone for a long time, she would prob-ably be thinking about settling down with them. That meant it was important that whoever she chose didn't make things difficult for her.

"The angel has a really mature way of thinking about things, huh?" one of the other boys commented.

"Well, I think Shiina's got a point," Amane mumbled. When everyone turned to look at him, he gave a strained smile. "It would be hard to spend time with somebody if their values didn't align with yours, and everyone wants to have someone by their side who accepts them, right? Even if you tried to get along with someone who held different values, eventually it would put too much stress on the rela-tionship, and you'd break up. I think that logically, taking that into account from the start is better."

Things would be even worse if your partner was the kind of person who couldn't tolerate differing opinions. The resulting stress would obviously hurt the relationship. So when it comes to dating someone with incompatible beliefs, it'd be best not to even bother.

"You've got a strict way of thinking about it... I can't even imagine what your type is, Fujimiya."

Amane shrugged. "Well, like everyone else, I'd prefer someone kind."

"That's such a vague answer! There's no other criteria?"

"I don't know what to say," he replied. "...Assuming that I get along with her, I think I'd like a girl who's gentle and sensible."

"By that standard, you would like most girls."

"Oh, shut up. Do you have some sort of problem with that?"

"It's not that I have a problem, but it just feels like a very common opinion."

"...All right, how about I say that whatever girl I fall for will be my preferred type? Whoever I like is my type at that moment."

Amane was afraid that if he gave too many specifics, he would end up revealing who he liked, so he kept his answers as vague as possible to arousing any suspicion. From behind him, he heard someone let out a small giggle.

"What an unexpectedly sweet thing for you to say."

His body stiffened at the sound of a familiar voice.

Amane wanted to ask her why she was over here and what exactly she had heard, but Mahiru coming over to his group wasn't particularly strange, nor was it weird that she would overhear what he said once she got close, so he swallowed his protests.

Keeping a stony expression so as not to betray his feelings, Amane didn't even look in Mahiru's direction as he responded, "Sorry."

Amane knew that it didn't give a very good impression to be so blunt with the class angel, but since he already had a reputation for being unsociable, nobody acted especially surprised.

"Shiina…"

"I'm sorry for showing up so late. I haven't been able to come over here much, but…are there any parts that you're having trouble understanding?"

Mahiru had finally finished up on the other side of the room and made her way over to check on Amane's group. She sounded quite apologetic. Amane didn't know whether she was standing next to him on purpose or not, but it wasn't good for his heart.

After the boys all looked at each other, one of them spoke up, looking sheepish.

"Uh, actually, we got Fujimiya to tutor us. We should be the ones apologizing, for joining your study session so suddenly."

"Oh, no, it's all right. It's my fault, really, for agreeing to tutor so many people without thinking about how much I can handle. I just couldn't keep up with everyone. But I'm relieved to hear that you got help from Fujimiya." She gave him a friendly smile and added, "Studying is one of Fujimiya's strong points."

Amane felt extremely uncomfortable, but he didn't show his discomfort. "I am honored by the compliment," he replied stoically.

Immediately after he said it, he looked up apologetically at Mahiru, worried that his comment might have sounded sarcastic, but Mahiru met his eyes with a smile and an affectionate look, as if to say that she understood everything.

"Fujimiya is very helpful and good at teaching, you know," Mahiru insisted.

"I…uh…I wouldn't really say that…," Amane stammered.

"Oh, and what would you call this? Plus, it's easy to see the way you support Chitose and Akazawa, too. You act cold, but you're always watching out for them, right? You extend your hand as soon as you see someone's in trouble."

Amane scowled when she said that it was *"easy to see"* him doing that, with such a gentle expression on her face.

Mahiru did sometimes compliment Amane, but he never expected her to say something like that or praise him in a place like this. His eyes began to dart nervously around the room.

"He's blushing, he's blushing!" Itsuki jeered.

"Shut up, Itsuki... It's totally normal to support your friends."

Mahiru smiled fondly at him. "I'm glad that it's become a normal thing for you."

Finally, Amane couldn't endure it any longer, and he turned away.

Under the desk, Itsuki kicked him lightly with the toe of his shoe, as if urging Amane on toward something.

As the study session concluded, Amane rolled his shoulders gently to loosen up the stiffness that had gradually accumulated there.

Mahiru was looking at him with her usual smile and a hint of deep affection—it was a look only someone close to her would recognize. Itsuki had noticed and started pestering Amane secretly under the desk again. The boys in their study group had also gotten used to Amane's presence and chatted openly with him as well.

For better or worse, Amane was exhausted. It was a good thing to have made some friendly acquaintances, but it was somewhat difficult to do anything at all with Mahiru there.

The other boys were finished studying too and returned the copies of Amane's notes with promises of candy and junk food to repay him for the help.

Some of their classmates had left partway through, either because they had other things to do or because it was a more serious study session than they wanted, so Amane was secretly admiring the ones who had stayed for their diligence.

"Sorry for making you wait. And after you helped me out, too."

Mahiru stayed to the very end, to clean and tidy the classroom and return the key to the office. Other classmates had asked if she wanted to head home together, but as the organizer, she had various tasks to finish up, so she'd given them each a firm refusal and had been about to stay behind alone until Amane had stepped in. He told her that they had all used the classroom together, and it would surely be dangerous to let Mahiru head home on her own late at night, so he would stay with her.

He wished that Itsuki and Chitose had been there to stay behind as well, though. He felt some minor frustration toward his friends, who had thoughtlessly ducked out earlier, as he and Mahiru walked down the deserted hallways together.

Since club activities were temporarily on hold, and since the sun had already set, there were probably only a few teachers, office staff, and students left in the building. It wasn't good to be seen alone with Mahiru at school, but it was too late to change that.

"No, no, I'm the one who should be apologizing," Amane insisted. "I might have gotten in your way instead."

"Not at all; you really helped me out," Mahiru replied. "There was no way I could go around to everyone by myself. I never imagined so many people would show up...and there were some people who joined at the last minute, so there were way more than I expected."

"I feel like that's not a big surprise, for the angel."

"...Oh, come on."

She shot him a look as a reminder that she didn't want him to call her by that nickname, which Amane let pass with feigned ignorance. It was his meager payback for her publicly complimenting him.

"But it went well; everyone tackled the material seriously," she said.

"There was a lot of chitchat throughout the room, but everyone was more serious than I expected. Even I was working hard to keep up."

"You always take your studies seriously, Fujimiya. You seem even more motivated for this round of exams than you have before."

"...I guess. I've been thinking I should put some more effort into certain things."

Amane intended to do the best he could at studying and at exercise. At the moment, there was hardly anyone around, and he had a good reason to be accompanying Mahiru, so he stayed by her side. However, Amane wanted to become someone who could be with her without needing a reason and not worry about people talking.

Mahiru, who he was sure had no idea of the deeper reasons behind Amane's efforts, smiled at him and said, "How admirable." They had just arrived at the entry hall, and she turned to look at their surroundings. "The sun's already gone down, hasn't it?"

"Sure has," Amane agreed.

He noticed her staring at him.

She wasn't wearing her usual angelic smile, but rather the more intimate and slightly expectant one that she often showed him when they were alone together.

Amane hesitated, briefly unsure of what she wanted. Though from their previous conversations, he managed to guess what she was thinking and put on a slight smile.

"...It's late, so I'll walk you home."

Evidently, he guessed correctly, because Mahiru's porcelain cheeks flushed slightly, turning the color of roses, and her lips gently curled up.

"Thank you for being so thoughtful," she said. "It's very kind of you."

"Are you making fun of me? You basically just told me what to do...," he muttered quietly.

"Heh-heh."

Apparently Mahiru had heard what he said, and she crinkled her eyes like she found it funny. "You dummy," she teased, before changing her shoes and heading out the front door. Since they were supposed to be walking together, Amane slowed down to match Mahiru's pace and let out a deliberate sigh.

...*I bet it's pretty obvious.*

It was clear that he had stayed behind so late in order to wait for Mahiru so that she wouldn't have to go home alone.

Only, it wasn't good for them to be alone together in public, so he had intended to walk behind or ahead of her, not side by side. Except now that she had anticipated it and manipulated him into escorting her, there was no way he could say no to her.

"...You're a girl, Miss Shiina, so you shouldn't go home too late, you know."

"How kind of you to say so. Usually, I get home safely, and today I have you with me, Mr. Fujimiya, so I feel extra safe."

"...Indeed."

Illuminated by the dim, unreliable streetlights, Mahiru's smile looked brighter than the bulbs themselves, and Amane averted his eyes to avoid being dazzled.

Chapter 5

Studying with Everyone

"Good morning, Fujimiya!"

"Morning."

The boys who had been in Amane's study group the day before greeted him breezily the following morning. Incidentally, Mahiru had been in high spirits the whole walk home and the rest of the night after they got back to their apartments.

Amane returned his classmates' morning greetings with a slight wave and set his bag down at his desk. Itsuki and Yuuta, who had both arrived before Amane, ambled over, smiling. Itsuki seemed to have a touch of Chitose's wicked scheming about him, and Amane didn't think it was his imagination.

Predictably, Itsuki's grin changed to a smug smirk. Amane almost clicked his tongue in irritation.

"How'd yesterday go?" Itsuki asked.

"Nothing really to report. And definitely nothing to warrant that dumb grin."

"Oh right, you guys had that study session, didn't you?" Yuuta said. "I had something else to do, so I couldn't make it. Did anything happen?"

Yuuta hadn't been there, so he didn't seem to know the reason behind Itsuki's smug expression.

Amane didn't feel like going to the trouble of explaining, so he shrugged and made a face at Itsuki that conveyed mostly annoyance and frustration. "No, not really. We just had a normal, solid study session."

"Oh, come on...," Itsuki prodded. "Nothing to say about my brilliant setup?"

"It was none of your business anyway, that's for sure."

Amane had been planning to escort Mahiru home (really, since their destinations were basically the same, it would be more accurate to say he was also going home) regardless of whether Itsuki had left first or not. Amane probably wouldn't have felt so awkward or been so worried about attracting attention, and it would have obviously been more comfortable if Itsuki and Chitose had tagged along.

"I'm fine," Amane insisted. "I'm making steady progress at my own pace, and I don't need any encouragement."

"I'm pushing you because I'm starting to get impatient, though...," Itsuki whined.

"Shut up. Or I won't let you copy my notes."

"Ah! This is where I must withdraw. I shall spare you this time."

"You're infuriating."

Itsuki was the one in trouble, now that exams were drawing near and there was no more time left. Itsuki would probably do fine even without much studying, but he had said himself that it would be impossible for him to pass any of his weak subjects without at least some preparation.

When Amane took the copy of notes out of his file folder and handed them over, he teased, "Victory is mine," but was doubtful whether Itsuki would study hard once he got home.

Amane went to give copies of his notes to the boys who had

greeted him earlier—they had requested them the day before. As thanks, they gave him candy until his hands were full.

"You're a very caring dude," Itsuki remarked as Amane returned to his desk carrying heaps of snacks. Itsuki seemed like he was about to launch into a story about Mahiru's praise for Amane the day before.

Amane could feel his face begin to twitch as he cut Itsuki off— "You didn't offer me anything, so I just made your copy along with the others."

Yuuta had been watching with a smile as always, but suddenly he made a disappointed face. "I should have participated yesterday. It sounds like it was pretty fun. I wanted to study with everyone, too."

"Well, Itsuki had fun messing with me," Amane said, "but I didn't have any fun being messed with."

"This again?"

"Now, now. Itsuki's teasing comes from a place of love," Yuuta jested. "Probably. I think."

"Why must you all doubt me so?"

"He gets sullen sometimes when you tease him too much, and it makes me wonder whether there's love behind the jokes or not. You've got to dial it back at times, you know? Fujimiya will probably forgive you eventually, but you'd better figure out where the line is before you cross it."

"Yeah, sure, no problem. I know exactly where the line is."

"This guy pisses me off," Amane muttered.

Itsuki had never teased Amane to the point of crossing any lines or making him truly angry. Even if Amane pouted a little bit, he was never really offended, and Itsuki always stopped when Amane clapped back in irritation, and he never complained when he got a particularly pointed retort, either. He probably knew where the line was.

Itsuki's knack at dancing around that line was impressive and a singular point of irritation in Amane's life.

"Well now, I suppose Itsuki has always been a little…irritating," Yuuta admitted.

"How can you be so casually cruel, Yuuta? Who knew you were such a harsh critic?"

"I've recently decided that I can stand to be a bit harsh with you sometimes."

"You monster! I protest!"

"Ah-ha-ha!"

Yuuta laughed it off as Itsuki faked a pose of indignation; it was obvious that he wasn't actually upset. Amane felt satisfied to see Itsuki on the receiving end of the jokes for once, on several levels.

Amane couldn't hate him, even at times like this, so he secretly had on a wry smile.

"So let's just set Itsuki aside for a moment…," Yuuta said.

"Don't leave me out!" he protested.

"We won't get anywhere with you jabbering on, Itsuki, so be quiet for a minute. Now, Amane, I'd also like to study together, the three of us. Want to have a study session on Saturday or Sunday?"

Itsuki obediently shut his mouth tight like a certain cartoon rabbit, and Yuuta turned away from him to ask Amane again, "How about it?"

Amane didn't have anything in particular planned for the weekend, and he figured that with Yuuta there, it would probably be a normal study session, so he was inclined to agree, but then he hesitated.

Amane thought a study session sounded fine, but there was the question of where to hold it.

"…So where would we do it?"

"Ah, my place is out," Itsuki responded. "My parents will be there, so I think it'll be awkward, or there might be an unpleasant atmosphere." Itsuki's tone was casual, but Amane could tell that his friend was upset about the poor relationship he had with his parents.

"...My house would be fine, I guess, but my older sisters will probably get in our way a little, so I don't think it's well-suited for studying," Yuuta said.

"You've got sisters?"

"Yeah, two of them. They're kind of loud, pushy people, so I think Fujimiya would probably be uncomfortable."

Amane knew that Yuuta was probably not downplaying it or anything, that his sisters really were those kinds of girls. If he had to guess, Amane got the feeling that they were the type he couldn't handle, so he thought it best to avoid Yuuta's house if possible.

That meant Amane's place would be the most convenient.

Itsuki had been to his apartment many times before, and Amane didn't have any objections to the idea of Yuuta coming in. At the same time, Amane wasn't the only person who spent time in that apartment.

Mahiru wasn't necessarily always in his apartment, but she was kind enough to come over and cook, and they had been studying together a lot recently, so there was a high probability that she would be there over the weekend.

Amane smiled vaguely, thinking that he'd better not bring guests over without getting Mahiru's permission first.

"Do you think you could ask her about it?" Itsuki asked.

"Ah, sure, I can do that." Amane nodded. "We can't just barge in without warning."

"It is your little love nest, after all...."

"Seriously, shut your mouth."

Amane glared at Itsuki, wondering what he would do if they were overheard, but Itsuki had kept his voice low enough, and none of their classmates seemed to be looking their way.

Amane gave an exasperated sigh and cast his eyes downward, thinking of Mahiru, who was not currently in the classroom.

✳   ✳   ✳

"Hey, Mahiru? I'm going to have a study session at my place with Itsuki and Kadowaki tomorrow morning. Is that all right?"

After dinner, as he was carrying the dishes over to the sink, Amane posed the question to Mahiru, who was carrying the silverware.

Itsuki had said that Saturday was better for his schedule. Amane felt bad about asking at the last minute.

Mahiru blinked dramatically once, then gave him an encouraging look.

"I don't mind. Should I make food for everyone?"

"Oh, I would feel bad asking you to do so much, but...but I'd be grateful if you could... Is that all right?"

"It's just a matter of making a bit more. I don't mind," she answered casually.

Amane was certain that it would still take a lot of extra labor. She'd probably planned on making lunch for herself anyway, but nevertheless, he wouldn't be able to thank Mahiru enough for adjusting her plans to match up with his.

"Can I study with you, too?"

"If you want to, the guys said it was fine... Should we call Chitose, too? I don't know whether she's free or not, or whether she's really going to study, but I feel a little anxious about leaving her out."

Chitose wasn't very studious. It wasn't that she didn't know how to study, but Amane certainly wouldn't call her an academic. Though she had participated in the previous day's study session, apparently, she hadn't made much progress, and she had even laughed about how she was going to fail the tests.

"You don't need to worry about that. I've already invited her."

"Huh?"

"Well, she was saying that she'll get told off by her father if she doesn't get a good score, for her anyway, on this round of tests, so just today, I made plans to study with her on Saturday."

"Maybe joining us was Chitose's plan all along?"

Amane had a feeling that Itsuki had told Chitose about their study party, but he had no definitive proof. He smiled wryly at the thought of his two meddling friends, convinced that she had gotten her information through Itsuki.

Wishing they had just told him the plan from the start, he quickly rinsed the oily plates in hot water and began washing the dishes. Mahiru giggled a little and started packing the cooled leftovers away in Tupperware.

"Well, whether that was her original aim or not, it looks like it will be a very lively study session, huh?" she remarked.

"Will that be all right for you? If it gets a bit loud?"

"I'll be fine," Mahiru insisted. "Besides, I've been studying every day, so I'm not that anxious about the tests."

Mahiru didn't need to worry, because she worked hard every day, so Amane didn't really think anything more of it.

Though he did wonder how the group was going to manage to study efficiently.

"Hey, Mahiru, after we're done, could I look at your notes?"

"Sure, I don't mind. But you take nice notes too, Amane. They're popular, I hear."

"My notes are, sure. I guess because they're fairly neat. But I'm curious about the notes of the top-ranking student."

"Don't get your hopes up because they're not as good as you're expecting."

Mahiru giggled again and put the leftovers in the refrigerator.

They would become Amane's breakfast the next day, so as he did the washing up, in his mind, he thanked Mahiru. He was able to eat her home cooking not only for dinner, but even for breakfast, improving his daily life, knowing that he was eating healthily every day.

"Amane, you're studying really hard for these exams, aren't you?"

"Well, I'd like to improve my confidence in a few areas, and I figure if I'm going to go to the trouble of studying, I should really work hard at it. I'd like to score in the top ten."

"Is that so...? All right, then how about I give you a little motivation, then?"

"Motivation?"

"If you do make it into the top ten, I'll do anything you ask."

"...Huh?"

Amane froze for a second and nearly dropped the plate he was holding into the sink. He couldn't believe what he'd just heard.

Almost breaking one of Mahiru's favorite plates brought Amane back to his senses, and he took a deep breath.

Then he glanced over beside him and saw Mahiru, wearing her usual placid smile, snapping the lid onto one of the containers.

"I said before that I would do basically anything if you just asked, but I figure this time, we can make it a real prize. I'll grant you any wish, even something you would never normally ask, okay?"

"...Girls shouldn't say things like that."

"Oh, are you going to ask me to do something dangerous?"

Though she must have been entirely aware that Amane would never do any such thing, Mahiru tilted her head teasingly as she asked, and Amane couldn't help but frown. She seemed confident that there would be no great danger in anything that Amane might request.

When Amane stared at Mahiru, she gave him a bemused smile and bounced over to stand beside him. He couldn't tell whether it was his imagination, but a hopeful look seemed to have flashed across her face.

"…Supposing I did ask for something dangerous, what would you do?"

"Well, that would depend on what it was, but I think…I would admire your chivalry and probably grant your wish."

It sounded like Mahiru did mean to fulfill Amane's request. Of course, that was probably because she was sure that he wouldn't force her to do anything unreasonable. Amane felt somewhat conflicted.

He didn't want to force her to do anything she didn't want to, but hearing the girl he liked tell him that she would do anything he wanted gave him all sorts of wild ideas—none of which he could say out loud.

He took a quick look at Mahiru and saw her smiling as if to say she was ready for anything. She looked so innocent. Amane felt skewered by his own wretchedness.

"…All right, I want you to let me lie in your lap, like you did before."

Amane just barely held it together. After some deliberation, he made up his mind and asked for something that he knew Mahiru was likely to agree to, and that he would in general never request.

He wanted to experience that pleasant feeling one more time. It didn't seem like an outrageous request, and Amane figured he could keep ahold of himself.

The moment he said it, Amane felt miserably embarrassed at his own request. Mahiru looked back at him, blinking repeatedly, and stared at Amane's face.

Then, with an adorable, bashful look, she answered, "Okay by me. I'll throw in an ear cleaning for you, so prepare to be pampered."

She puffed out her chest, looking like she had no doubt Amane would make it into the top ten.

＊   ＊   ＊

"We're here!"

The Saturday before the tests, as planned, Itsuki, Chitose, and Yuuta showed up around ten in the morning, called out a greeting in unison from the doorway, and shuffled over the threshold.

Apparently, the three of them had grown up in the same neighborhood, and it had been convenient for them to meet up before coming over. They met up first also because Yuuta didn't know where Amane's apartment was, but the main reason was probably because they were already good friends.

Amane welcomed them. "Great, come on in."

"Where's Mahiru?" Chitose asked.

"In the kitchen, getting lunch ready."

So that they didn't have to worry about their midday meal, Mahiru had come over to Amane's apartment ahead of time to prepare it. She had made a trip to a supermarket that opened early in the morning to buy the ingredients.

She was making roast beef and wanted to let it slowly cook so that by lunch, it would be just the right tenderness and ready to eat.

"...You two are getting awfully comfortable...," Itsuki whispered.

"Shut up."

"You guys are like a newlyweds, welcoming your colleagues over for a meal."

"One more word, and you won't get any lunch," Amane threatened.

"No way! I'm eating Mahiru's cooking!"

Warning Itsuki to keep his mischief to a minimum, Amane looked over at Yuuta, who was staring at him, slightly astonished.

"What's up, Yuuta?"

"...It's just, Shiina seems so at home here in your apartment, Fujimiya," he replied.

"…It'd almost be weirder if she wasn't," Amane grumbled. "…Since she's always making food for me."

Amane turned away abruptly and saw Itsuki grinning with his hands over his mouth. It reminded him of the way his mother smiled, which made him angry, and he kicked Itsuki lightly in the shin.

"Welcome, everyone…," Mahiru said as she emerged from the kitchen. "Oh, Akazawa, what happened?"

Amane scoffed. "Don't worry about him."

Mahiru looked worried about Itsuki, who seemed to be wearing a mysterious smile. It wasn't anything she needed to worry about, and Amane wished she would just ignore it.

Mahiru seemed to conclude that Itsuki's expression was nothing to be concerned about, so even though she still looked curious, she put on her usual smile and returned to the kitchen with a flutter of her apron. "I've got a little more preparation to do in there, so please go ahead into the living room."

Watching her leave, Itsuki mumbled, "She is absolutely brimming with just-married wife energy." This time, Amane slapped him on the back.

They waited for Mahiru to finish her work in the kitchen, and after she was done, she brought out tea. "Well, should we get to studying?" she asked, taking a seat next to Amane. The other three had made sure to leave that spot open.

"Yeah!"

"All right, what parts don't you understand, Chitose? We covered English yesterday and were planning to work on math today, right?"

"Everything," Chitose replied.

Mahiru balked. "E-everything…?"

"Chi is not very good at math," Itsuki commented. "She barely avoided failing last time."

Chitose wasn't completely hopeless, but that was her weakest sub-ject, and she announced after every test that only divine intervention had kept her from failing.

The word *"everything"* caused Mahiru's cheek to twitch slightly, but since math was Chitose's weakness, there really was no helping it. They would be lucky if she managed to understand the basics.

"She has a hard time with applied problems, so the best thing would be to show her how to use the formulas with each exercise, I think," Itsuki said.

"Is she all right on the formulas?" Mahiru asked Itsuki.

"...You're okay there, right?" Itsuki asked Chitose.

"Probably." Chitose nodded.

Amane got the feeling that Chitose was not actually okay, and that Mahiru had her work cut out for her. Chitose wasn't exactly dumb; she just couldn't solve the problems because she didn't know how to use the formulas. So as long as she learned how, she ought to be able to get a decent score, for her anyway.

"You almost seem motivated now, Itsuki," Amane observed.

"Ha-ha-ha!"

"Don't try to laugh it off; get to studying."

Why do you think we organized this study session? Amane thought to himself.

"Yuuutaaa, Amane's being mean!" Itsuki whined playfully.

"You'd better shape up soon, then."

With a bright smile, Yuuta refused to rescue Itsuki, who let his shoulders droop dejectedly.

Yuuta himself had already studiously opened his textbook and notebook to get started. Amane wished that Itsuki and Chitose would follow his example.

Yuuta didn't seem to have any particularly weak subjects. He was an outstanding student who had above-average scores across the board.

Amane also wasn't worried about any subject in particular—all he had left was to polish up his memorization and application skills.

He entrusted the task of tutoring Chitose to Mahiru and lowered his gaze to the world history textbook that he had set out for himself.

Amane and the others continued studying after lunch, but eventually, around mid-afternoon, Chitose seemed to reach the limits of her concentration and leaned back in her chair. "I'm exhausted! Hey, Amane, could we play a video game?"

"You're free to play if you want, but I can't make any promises about your grades…"

"Geez, you're so strict."

"It's because you never just play a little bit. If you think you can control yourself, then I suppose you can go ahead," he replied while solving a workbook problem, signaling that he was going to continue studying. Out of the corner of his eye, he saw Chitose puff out her cheeks a little.

Amane had predicted it was only a matter of time before Chitose got bored of studying, an activity he knew she hated. That was why he had put four controllers and several games beside the console in his TV stand.

A human's attention span can only last so long, so he figured it wouldn't be so bad for his friends to play and take a breather.

On the other hand, Amane had no problem studying some more. Since they started, he took a short break every hour, and in the first place, he didn't mind studying. He could keep going for quite a long time if he wanted to.

"You're no fun, Amane!" Chitose huffed.

"This is supposed to be a study party, right? I guess it's fine if you really want to play. I've got four controllers, so how about you take a short break?"

"Okay, I'll accept your offer, but…you shouldn't push yourself too hard, okay?"

"I've been taking breaks."

"What a dedicated student! You've always been so serious, Amane. All right, then, I'm gonna game. Let's play, Itsuki."

"Yeah, sure. But we can't waste all of our time."

Amane was not surprised that Itsuki also seemed tired after the three or so hours of studying and was keen to play a game.

"Wanna join, Yuuta?" he asked.

"Sure, why not? Is it all right, Fujimiya?"

"Mmm." Amane nodded.

Even Yuuta, who was more serious about his studies than Itsuki or Chitose, was showing interest in taking a short break. Amane confirmed that Yuuta was free to join the others, then looked back down at his workbook.

Beside him, Mahiru was quietly working on solving a set of problems. She was as focused as before and showed no signs of stopping.

"You're not going to play, Mahiru?" he asked her.

"I'm going to study a little more," Mahiru replied.

"I see."

Amane had vowed to start taking his studies seriously, which was the only reason he wasn't stopping, but Mahiru had a natural affinity for studying, and he couldn't help but admire her diligence.

She'd probably continue ranking first place on the exams since she never failed to put in the effort—that dedication was just another reason why Mahiru was so incredible.

After watching the other three excitedly get up from the table and start taking up positions in front of the television, Amane put them out of his mind and went back to work. He could hear pencil lead scratching against paper, the sound of the eraser rubbing out the marks, and, very clearly, the sound of Mahiru's breathing at his side.

While listening half-heartedly to the animated voices of his friends nearby, Amane focused on remembering which questions the teachers tended to choose for exams. Several of his teachers had been teaching him since his first year of high school, and he knew that those teachers' tests were relatively easy. And from their personalities and the way they conducted their classes, he could guess what sections of the material they would pull from, especially since he remembered their style from the previous year. Amane felt pretty certain that he could predict what they would put on their tests.

He had even told Chitose about which sections of the textbook the test questions would most likely cover. It was just a calculated guess, but he had never been wrong before, so if she prioritized those areas when she studied, she would probably at least avoid failing.

"Amane, here."

While he was solving problems in silence, Mahiru had stood up unnoticed, and now she set a cup of coffee down in front of him.

He smiled at the beverage, which he guessed had one small sugar cube and a single portion of milk stirred in.

"The usual is all right, yeah?"

"Mm. Thank you."

They had been spending time together for half a year, so they had gotten to know each other's tastes.

Feeling grateful toward Mahiru, who had brought the coffee over right when he started to get a craving, Amane wrapped his fingers around the mug handle, then realized that she had also placed a small plate before him.

"What's this?"

"A *financier*. I baked them yesterday, thinking we would need some sugar to fuel our brains."

On the little plate sat one bite-sized *financier*, baked to a perfect golden brown. A toothpick stuck out of the top of the small cake, so that he could pick it up without getting his fingers dirty. Mahiru had probably made them bite-size so that they could be enjoyed in the spare moments between studying.

Mahiru had also dutifully set out cakes for Itsuki and the others still playing the video game. Theirs were slightly larger and served on plates that sat together on a platter.

Mahiru had also prepared coffee for the three of them, but the milk and sugar were self-serve, with sugar packets and little pots of cream laid out on the platter.

With a smile, she quietly approached the gamers and set the tray down on a table nearby. "You should all have some, too."

"Wow! Thank you, Mahiru!"

"Oh, snacks! Perfect timing, too. Thank you, Shiina."

"It's nothing, really."

Mahiru returned to the table, gazing happily at the trio now enjoying their snack time, and Amane felt his lips curling into a smile as well.

"...I sort of feel like I made you prepare a lot of stuff."

"No, I did it because I wanted to," Mahiru insisted. "And I did everything in between studying, so it was a good way to take breaks."

"You're the type of person who always goes all out, seriously."

"...I just use my time on the people I want to use it on."

Amane felt a hot lump rising up in his throat when she mumbled these words in a quiet voice.

He washed it down with a swig of coffee. Mahiru hadn't added any extra sugar, but it somehow seemed particularly sweet.

The sweetness wasn't unpleasant, and he wasn't sure how he should respond to what Mahiru had said, so Amane stared back down at his workbook, to fool himself into thinking he had nothing to say.

In the end, the gaming tournament lasted well into the evening.

Amane eventually took a break from his studies and joined in, too, when he found that he could no longer focus. Except it wasn't just the fatigue of hours of study that affected Amane's concentration.

What did she mean, she uses her energy on the people she wants to use it on?

Amane had been replaying Mahiru's quiet murmuring over and over again in his head. He had always known that Mahiru did things for the people she liked, but when she put it that way, it sounded like she held some special affection for Amane.

Amane certainly thought that Mahiru liked him, but his understanding was that it wasn't in a romantic way.

The way she'd said that made him wonder if she was doing everything because she liked him, not as a friend... His mind was running wild with the idea.

I mean, I would understand if she was doing all this work because I'm such a failure of a human being, and she felt like she just had to step in, but...

In fact, Amane was bad enough at housework that he couldn't rule out the possibility. He could survive on his own, if he really tried, but he did rely on Mahiru a lot.

He couldn't decide whether Mahiru just wanted to look after him, or whether she was being overly caring because she was into him. Given his feelings for her, Amane would have liked to imagine that it was the latter, and he didn't think that it was completely hopeless. However, he still had serious doubts about whether he was the kind of person Mahiru could ever actually love.

"...Amane? You fell out of the ring."

"Huh...?"

Amane had gotten lost in thought in the middle of a game, and unknowingly let his character go out of bounds. Since he didn't have any more lives left, he was knocked out of the game.

A close match unfolded between Itsuki, Chitose, and Yuuta. Amane hadn't expected Yuuta to be so good at video games.

Normally, Amane would never make such an obvious mistake. That was how distracted he was by Mahiru's comment.

"Your concentration must really be shot from studying, Amane. You're spaced out."

"...Must be," Amane agreed. "Mahiru, you want in on the next game?"

"No, I've got to get dinner ready soon, so..."

Mahiru glanced at the clock, and when Amane followed her gaze, he saw that it was just short of seven o'clock. It was probably a little bit late to start dinner preparations.

"Oh, she's right, it's already so late... I've got to get going. I can't stay over, after all," Chitose said.

"Yeah, I'm sure you would have liked to stay at Shiina's place, Chi, but we didn't bring you a change of clothes or anything. Plus, you didn't ask, and I doubt you would fit into any of her clothes, after all..."

"Tell me, my darling Itsuki, just what do you mean by that?"

"I'm talking about your heights, of course, yes."

Mahiru giggled as she watched the couple cheerfully bicker, as they always did. "Come over and stay next time."

"You sure?"

"I'm sure. As long as you tell me ahead of time."

"Well then, I'll stay over at Amane's at the same time," Itsuki added.

Amane frowned. "I have a feeling you're just angling for a meal..."

"You got me. Her cooking is just too delicious!" Itsuki laughed, with no ill intent.

With a sigh, Amane told him, "You know you've got to ask Mahiru, right?"

Mahiru would be the one who had to make all the extra food, so Amane couldn't very well volunteer her.

If she didn't agree, then the boys could eat out or get convenience store food, which would feel more like a party anyway, so it wouldn't be the worst thing.

Mahiru nodded her approval with a smile, and Amane had a feeling Chitose and Itsuki would be staying over soon.

"Will Kadowaki be coming next time, too?" Mahiru asked.

"Oh, could I?"

"Well…," Amane began.

"If you come, let's have a 'kick Amane's butt into gear' party!" Itsuki interrupted.

"Hey, where do you get off planning weird parties?"

"Come on, how 'bout it?"

Amane's cheek twitched as Itsuki put on a broad grin. Yuuta was taken aback for a moment but then smiled with relief.

"Hey, Mahiru? …What did you mean when you said that you use your energy on the people you want to use it on?"

While they were standing in the entryway after seeing everybody else off, Amane falteringly asked her the question that had been weighing on his mind all evening.

He had been wavering over whether to ask her about it, but he had been grumbling about not knowing what to do as Itsuki left, and Itsuki had given him a little kick and said, "Don't worry about it, man, just ask."

Amane hadn't been expecting a literal "kick in the butt," so he'd smacked Itsuki in retaliation. Itsuki hadn't seemed particularly likely to learn his lesson, so it had felt like a futile gesture.

Mahiru blinked at Amane. Slowly, the corners of her mouth curled into a smile. "…What do you think I meant?"

"Like, that you can't let this useless guy out of your sight for a minute?"

Amane was too self-conscious to say anything rash, as he didn't want to come off as arrogant.

"Heh-heh, well, that's true. I'm afraid to take my eye off you. If I wasn't here, you'd really be in trouble."

"I can't argue with that."

Mahiru truly did take extremely good care of him. If she wasn't around, Amane would never be able to maintain his current lifestyle.

"...It's fine, you know? I like taking care of you, Amane."

"I'd let myself go to pieces...without you, I'd fall apart and wither away..."

"Heh-heh."

The frightening thing about Mahiru was that Amane knew that if she left, his whole life would become an emotional wreck.

In several senses, he had become something like her prisoner. It would be impossible for him to leave her—and he didn't want to. Needless to say, the main reason was because he was in love with her.

If he were to confess his feelings and be rejected, he was sure he would feel like death, emotionally and physically. Amane laughed at himself but didn't tell her that was why he hadn't been able to move forward.

Mahiru stepped toward him, inexplicably. She didn't press up against him, but she was close enough that they were just lightly touching. She drew close to Amane until she was right in front of him and looked up—then with her index finger, she traced the outline of his lips.

"...I'm going to spoil you as much as I like, so just relax and enjoy it, okay?"

Mahiru narrowed her eyes impishly at Amane. He realized he'd forgotten how to breathe.

Mahiru was wearing a smile he had never seen before. It was sweet, yet provocative...even enchanting. It could even be called

devilish and was enough to bewitch anyone. Amane could feel it tug-
ging at his emotions.

He could also feel his heart pounding and the blood rushing
through his veins.

Amane had seen many of Mahiru's smiles, from her beautiful
angelic one, to a subtle, vanishing smirk, to a cherubic grin, but she
had never given him such a flirtatious look before.

She gazed with satisfaction at Amane, still frozen in place, then
reverted to her usual smile as she headed for the kitchen. "Well, I'm
going to go make dinner."

Amane watched her go, cheeks burning.

Chapter 6

Before the Test, a Moment

The Sunday before the start of exams, Amane was studying quietly in his own room.

He wanted to get high marks, but there was also another reason he was studying—he was trying to drive thoughts of Mahiru out of his head.

"...I'm going to spoil you as much as I like, so just relax and enjoy it, okay?"

Mahiru had whispered those unbelievable words with a devilish smile, and now thoughts of her threatened to fill his head, leaving room for nothing else.

Amane didn't know whether Mahiru's recent suggestive behavior toward him was intentional, but it was certainly effective. He appreciated it, but at the same time, it made him nervous.

Until he was sure of Mahiru's intentions, he couldn't really make a move.

All sorts of questions troubled him, so to drive them all away, he'd been studying furiously since early morning. His efforts were at least somewhat successful, because he'd gotten so caught up in the work that by the time he realized, it was past two in the afternoon.

The fact that he had worked straight through without eating lunch was proof of how focused he had been, but now that he had noticed the time and checked the clock, his stomach immediately growled with hunger.

"...I guess I should at least eat lunch."

Amane stretched out to relieve some of the stiffness that had built up after sitting in one place for so long. Then he stood up and left his room.

Mahiru had said she would be home alone studying for exams that day, and she hadn't come over to Amane's. That meant Amane would have to fix lunch on his own.

Thinking about how he'd been spoiled with good food since meeting Mahiru, he headed for the kitchen and opened the refrigerator.

He put a frozen portion of rice that had been set aside for quick use into the microwave, and while it was thawing, he took a bowl and scooped out several types of the preserved vegetables that Mahiru had prepared ahead of time, guaranteeing some color and nutrients for his meal.

All of this is Mahiru's doing.

If it had been just Amane, he wouldn't have prepared any vegetables. His lunch would've come from the convenience store.

Now he had a fair amount of food in the house, and he also knew how to make some things himself. They weren't on the same level as Mahiru's cooking, which was always delicious, lovely to look at, and nutritious to boot. Still, he had learned to make some edible dishes.

Using what he'd learned from Mahiru, Amane made a simple fried rice for lunch with just eggs and bacon. But the meal turned out to be plenty colorful thanks to the side dishes Mahiru had prepared.

With the addition of instant Chinese-style soup, it was a perfectly satisfactory menu for an easy lunch.

He loaded it all on a tray and carried it over to the dining table. "Let's eat."

He smiled softly as he looked down at a weekend lunch that he previously would have had trouble imagining. Then he pressed his hands together in thanks and picked up his spoon.

The fried rice that he brought to his mouth had a somewhat strong flavor, different from Mahiru's, but it wasn't bad. It turned out to be well seasoned for something prepared by a high school boy.

It's really different, huh?

Amane's eating habits had completely changed, and so had various other things about him. In all sorts of ways, he had become completely spoiled.

He wondered if he was becoming a better person in his daily life. After experiencing life with Mahiru, Amane didn't want to return to his previous existence—now that he knew life could be this good, he didn't want to go back. He had become really spoiled, in the sense that he felt he would never be satisfied if Mahiru left.

He wasn't only pampered in all practical aspects of life; he was spoiled emotionally as well.

Amane remembered something he had heard before from his father, Shuuto. Apparently, the Fujimiya men were the earnestly devoted type. The type who falls in love with only one person and then treasures them.

Amane did not have to think about whether he too had inherited those tendencies. Ever since he had become aware that he was in love with Mahiru, he paid even less attention to other girls. The most important thing was that he wanted to treasure Mahiru and make her happy.

…I won't settle for anyone but Mahiru.

Whether he was the one to bring her joy or not, as long as Mahiru was happy, he decided he would back off right away if she fell for someone else and chose that person instead. He told himself that seeing Mahiru smiling joyfully was enough.

However, he also had contradictory feelings. He really wanted to be the one to make her happy, and he definitely didn't want to give her away. He didn't want to be apart from Mahiru, and he liked being the only one who really knew her.

Some people would probably call what he was feeling an obsession—his heart was full of emotions that he could not explain to anyone else, like the feeling that he just couldn't live without Mahiru.

She wasn't just a pretty face; she had a pure heart as well. Amane had frankly been manipulated by the deep, strong feeling of love that was in his heart.

"...I wouldn't have so much trouble if I was more assertive."

Amane laughed a little. The words that he had muttered out loud naturally had a self-deprecating ring to them.

For the first time in his sixteen years of life, he was in love with someone, and he wanted to be the one by her side, but he had no idea how to make that happen.

Anyone else would probably have laughed, if they knew that he had made it to sixteen without experiencing his first love.

He was aware that he had a craven and cautious nature, and that he didn't know the first thing about approaching girls. He believed that these qualities had helped earn Mahiru's trust, and that they weren't things that he could change easily. But he had always wished that he could be more assertive.

That was exactly why he was working so hard at his studies and making an effort to exercise. He was trying to gain some self-confidence.

With a quiet, bitter smile, Amane scarfed down the rest of the fried rice.

*　　*　　*

Amane took a short break after eating to limber up his stiff muscles with some more stretching, and while he was at it, he decided to do some light exercise to relax. He changed into running clothes in his room.

He had been sitting at his desk for a while, so he figured a bit of physical activity would be a good change of pace.

Still, he didn't have that much stamina. He would need to reserve some energy for studying more later. He was sure that he would sleep like a log that night.

Reminding himself to be careful not to overdo it, Amane stepped through the door, and happened to meet Mahiru just as she was walking out of her own apartment.

"Ah, Amane... Going to exercise?"

She could clearly tell by his outfit. She gave him a charming smile, and he nodded in response. Mahiru was dressed like she was going out, so Amane figured he must have caught her just as she was leaving.

For a second, he remembered what had happened the day before and almost groaned out loud, but he had calmed down a little since then, so he didn't get flustered from just seeing her.

"Yeah, I need a break," he replied. "You too? Looks like you're going shopping."

"Yes. Speaking of which, I remember being low on eggs. I thought I'd make rolled omelets for dinner tonight. We've got exams tomorrow, and if I leave some for breakfast, they might help you do your best..."

"Seriously? Suddenly I feel a surge of energy!"

"I'm doing it for my sake, too, you know." Mahiru put a hand over her mouth and giggled a little.

Amane answered, frowning slightly, "I can't help myself; you make the best omelets."

This brought the conversation to a pause, but both knew that Amane wasn't actually upset. Through the gaps in Mahiru's fingers, he could see her smile widen.

"Ah, that's right, I used the last egg and also some bacon earlier. And I ate one of the frozen portions of rice."

"Oh, you made your own lunch?" Mahiru remarked. "Impressive."

"...I feel like you're making fun of me. I believe I do cook occasionally even when you're over."

Naturally, Amane felt bad about leaving all the cooking to Mahiru, so he usually tried to help her with simple tasks, and on days when Mahiru seemed to be tired or feeling down, he would take over and make the meals.

There were limits to what he could make, so sometimes the menu deviated considerably from what they had planned on. Disregarding the presentation and accepting that the flavor would be inferior to Mahiru's food, Amane was capable of cooking a passable meal.

So there was no reason for her to praise him like that just because he had made lunch.

"I know that, but you hardly ever do it when you're home alone, right? You tend to choose instant meals when you're by yourself, because cooking is a pain and you're fine with something easy."

"Uh—"

"Guessing from the ingredients and from your repertoire, I bet you made fried rice or something like that. It sounds like you did a good job, so that's great."

Amane was at a loss for words. She saw right through him. He thought he could feel his blood begin to boil.

Mahiru broke the tension when she laughed out loud and

extended a hand toward Amane. She gently combed her fingers through his hair, fluffing it up as she hit him with a charming smile.

Amane pursed his lips tightly. He didn't hate the feeling; rather, it made him happy. He really had become spoiled.

"…Knock it off already, geez."

"Aw, too bad. I wanted to do it more."

As she said that, Mahiru readily pulled away and smiled gently.

It occurred to Amane that his serious expression was only making things worse, and he turned away from her.

"…Are eggs the only thing you're buying?"

He changed the subject so that Mahiru couldn't pet him anymore.

"Let's see, there are other ingredients I need for dinner, like the eggs…and milk, but that should do it, I think. I was planning to make a quick trip, so I figured I'd just go to the closest grocery store."

"Got it. I can pick all that up on my way back home."

Amane wouldn't have said anything if Mahiru had other errands or shopping to do besides for groceries, things he couldn't do in her stead. But if she didn't have anything else to go out for, there was no reason for her to spend the extra time and effort.

Amane was going outside anyway, so it would be better to have her stay home and do something else she wanted to do. She spent time every night making him dinner, so he figured he should at least do this much.

"Huh? But then you'll have to carry it all."

"It's fine, I'll go shopping on my way back. And it's not like the grocery store is that far."

"Wh-what about money?"

"I've got my cash card with me. And I've already checked the balance. I can get a receipt from the supermarket, so there won't be any problem with splitting the bill or anything."

©Hanekoto

Amane cocked his head as to ask if there was anything else, and this time, Mahiru fumbled over her words.

"…Sorry to make you do this."

"I told you, it's fine; I'm going out anyway."

Amane ruffled Mahiru's hair in retaliation, and she looked at him with narrowed eyes as if he was tickling her. Something in her expression looked genuinely happy, and Amane was quietly relieved that he hadn't committed some grave mistake.

"…All right, I'll leave it to you. I'll be waiting at home."

"Whose home?"

"I wonder?"

Mahiru tilted her head slightly to the side, looking bashful. Then without missing a beat, she opened the door to Amane's apartment, using the spare key that she had been holding already, and slipped in smoothly through the crack.

Having made her answer obvious, Mahiru peeked back out through the door and smiled at Amane.

"See you when you get back, Amane."

"…I'm going now," he replied, feeling amused by Mahiru, who no longer seemed to care whose apartment was whose.

Mahiru's smile grew wider as she waved good-bye to Amane.

After warming up with some light stretching, Amane went for an easy jog that lasted a little less than an hour, and then made a trip to the supermarket as part of his cooldown before returning home.

Since he was jogging, he was able to relax and exercise without overthinking, and his mind quieted a little bit. For now, things seemed to have settled down without him having to respond to all of Mahiru's provocations, so he returned home feeling relieved. With the quiet shuffling of her house slippers, Mahiru came to greet him at the door.

"Welcome home. I went ahead and filled the bath with hot water. Want to get in?"

She casually took the shopping bags out of his hands, and he found himself gaping at her.

Itsuki and Yuuta had both said that she acted exactly like a newly-wed wife, and she really did. Mahiru herself probably didn't intend it that way, but her movements were brisk and efficient, and somebody who didn't know better might have made that assumption. Amane felt strangely embarrassed by the thought.

"...Amane?"

"Ah, it's nothing. Thank you, I will go take a bath."

He smiled vaguely in response to the strange look from Mahiru, rinsed his hands at the sink, then headed for his room to get ready for the bath.

He pulled out his usual loungewear, and then went into the bathroom, where, as Mahiru had said, the bathtub was full of piping hot water and set to the perfect temperature.

After saying a silent thanks to Mahiru for being so prepared and generally being there for him, he showered off the sweat from his run.

Amane was self-indulgent and lazy at heart, but that didn't mean he was okay with being dirty. He was someone who enjoyed a good bath.

When he submerged himself in the bathtub after properly washing the filth off his body and hair, it felt like all the fatigue in his mind and body melted away. He realized that he was pretty worn out as the exhaustion seemed to dissolve in the hot water.

As he soaked in the bathwater that was just the right temperature, Amane leaned back against the side of the tub and exhaled.

Then he looked down at his body through the clear water—he hadn't added bath salts or anything to it—and his exhale turned into a sigh.

"…Still got a lot of work to do, huh?"

It hadn't been very long since he'd started really exercising, so it was to be expected. Amane had very little muscle on his body because he had never trained and ate properly. He was extremely thin, a far cry from his image of masculinity. The words *bean sprout* came immediately to mind.

Amane wanted to get a little stronger and improve his looks while he was at it. Some of his classmates had seen him in his "mystery man" form before, so he couldn't heedlessly assume that look without attracting suspicion, but he knew that he could be more diligent with his skin care and grooming.

He admired Mahiru, who was never negligent in her daily self-care. He was sure that she must put in a lot of work that he wasn't even aware of.

As he thought about all these things, Amane felt a considerable drowsiness creep over him, probably from the comfortable warmth of the water and his own fatigue. He let out another deep sigh as he began dozing off in the tub.

Eventually, Mahiru, concerned that he was taking too long in the bath, ended up waking him in a panic when she opened the bathroom door to check on him.

"Um, you know…it's dangerous to stay in too long, okay?"

"I'm really sorry for being so careless."

All Amane could do was apologize earnestly. He wasn't sure whether Mahiru's flushed cheeks were due to anger or embarrassment from glimpsing his top half in the bath—he imagined it was at least partially from worry.

He had heard that people had drowned in as little as thirty centimeters of water, so Mahiru's anger seemed justified. Amane imagined that she was all the more anxious because she herself couldn't swim.

He tried to come up with some excuse, but his mind was in a fog.

He hadn't been completely asleep; really it was more like his consciousness was dipping a toe into the ocean of slumber. He was confident that he would have woken up without a problem if he had lost his balance and bumped into the side of the tub.

"...Why are you pushing yourself so hard?"

Amane felt instantly remorseful when he heard the suspicion in Mahiru's words. He could tell that he'd messed up when he heard the anxiety in her voice, which made it clear that he'd given her cause for stress.

"I won't deny the value of hard work," Mahiru continued, "but if you can't handle it all, shouldn't you ease up a little?"

"You're right, of course. I'll be more careful next time."

"But why are you doing all this, Amane?" she asked again.

"...I guess...because I want to become someone I can be proud of."

Even though she sounded a little angry, Mahiru looked mostly sad. Amane smiled meekly and stroked her head to try to wipe away the anxious look in her eyes, while vowing not to make such a mistake again.

"I've been thinking I wanna be more confident in myself, is all. And I wanted to start with things like my studies and exercise. I didn't mean to worry you; this was really all my fault. Next time, I'll keep in mind how much I can handle."

"...Are you in that big of a hurry?"

"I guess there's probably no rush, but I want to work harder... To make myself into someone I can be confident in. After all, I'm working hard for my own sake," Amane told her with a smile as he rubbed her head.

Mahiru stared hard into Amane's eyes, then sighed. "...I understand your determination. That said, I'm serious: If you don't take better care of yourself, I'm going to get really worried, okay?"

"I said I was sorry."

"But I think you really shine when you try so hard, and I don't want to get in the way of your progress. I've been watching you but trying not to get in your way."

"If anything, you're the one keeping me going," he insisted. "Taking care of meals is really a huge help. I can't manage that as well as you can, after all."

"You're the one putting in all the effort, so it would be more accurate to say that it's all I can do to help... Do your best, but don't push yourself too hard, okay?"

"I'll try not to make you worry again."

No doubt, he would be careful not to fall asleep in the bath again. He had no desire to learn what drowning felt like.

Amane also didn't want to make Mahiru fret and cry, so he decided to take better care of his physical health and not overexert himself.

Mahiru still looked a little skeptical, so he continued to try to reassure her by gently stroking her hair.

Chapter 7

After the Test, a Moment

Two days passed, and the tests were over. Amane felt liberated.

He surprisingly spent less time sitting at his desk during exams than when regular classes were in session, and he found that test prep was easier than his usual studies. Though this time around, there had been additional pressure, because he was more invested in the outcome.

Typically, Amane put in a reasonable amount of effort and always got a decent score. However, this time, he'd spent extra time studying and really focused on acing his exams. He'd been a bit nervous going into the tests, but now that they were over, he felt satisfied with his performance.

He had gotten together with Mahiru to compare their answers from the previous day's tests, and although he hadn't gotten a perfect score, it seemed like he had gotten a very good one. They would probably go over today's questions in detail once they got home, and Amane was confident that he had answered better this time around.

Amane leaned back against his chair and let his body relax as he took a break. Chitose staggered over, looking like she had been drained of all vitality.

"Amaneee, how'd it go?"

Her expression lacked its usual luster. Amane knew that Chitose was not a big fan of studying. She was a quick learner but not the kind of person to put in the work, and in this case, she didn't prepare enough.

"There wasn't anything specific that gave me trouble, so I think I did well," he answered.

"Wow, you were really serious about it this time. You gonna ask me how I did?"

"Let me guess, you did terribly but somehow avoided failing?"

"You got it."

"After all that tutoring, it'd be a shame if you still failed."

Compared to Itsuki and Chitose, and even Yuuta, Mahiru and Amane were far enough ahead in their studies that they had time to help Chitose so she could pass the tests.

Chitose's cheekiness and her attitude toward school often got in the way of her studies, but fundamentally, she had a good head on her shoulders and wasn't bad at understanding the material—so as long as it was taught well, she would grasp it quickly.

As for whether she would retain the information after the tests, that depended on whether she ever bothered to review it.

"It's fine, it's fine! I did better than ever before!" she said triumphantly.

"Glad to hear it. Not that the bar was all that high, but...as long as you're happy, I'm happy. Just remember to work hard at the end of the semester, too."

"Whaa—? We just finished these tests; don't talk about the next ones...that's depressing... Right now, I want to celebrate our freedom! Right, Itsuki?"

"That's right! We shouldn't spend the present dwelling on the past or thinking about some far-off future."

Itsuki, slumped listlessly in his chair behind Amane, groaned and agreed with what Chitose had said. Itsuki had obviously studied more seriously than Chitose, but the English exam had practically done him in, and he had no energy left.

"I want to compare my test answers with someone, though," Amane said.

"No way! Don't make us think about the tests anymore!"

Itsuki and Chitose clung to each other, looking absolutely exhausted, commiserating over their trials and tribulations.

"You seem lively enough to me," Amane grumbled, and shifted his gaze to the throng of people in the classroom who had finished their exams.

They were gathering one after another around Mahiru, probably to compare answers with her.

They wanted to see Mahiru's answers, since she had gotten nearly perfect scores on previous tests. With a humble smile, Mahiru pulled out her various answer sheets.

Amane had no desire to join the fray, so he would compare answers with her at home.

"…Must be tough."

He didn't call Mahiru by name, but it must have been clear who he meant.

Itsuki and Chitose both looked over at Mahiru and grinned.

"Well, the angel is cute, and clever, and popular, so she's in great demand."

"You could get in there too and help her out?"

"I don't see any need for that," he scoffed.

"Yeah, guess you're right."

"*Plus, you'll be there when she gets home*"—Itsuki didn't say that part out loud, but Amane knew the logical conclusion of that train of thought. He was grateful to his friend for not voicing it, but Itsuki's grinning face, which basically said he knew all about it, was more than enough to make Amane irritable.

Itsuki laughed again at Amane's scowl, and the lines in Amane's forehead grew deeper. Then he heard another voice laughing with amusement, and he relaxed his grimace just a little.

"Itsuki, if you tease him too much, Fujimiya will pout," Yuuta remarked.

"He's fine, he's fine, Amane won't get mad at me just for that."

"It looked like the vein in his temple was going to pop just now, though."

"Uh-oh, I think you're right."

Yuuta surprised Amane by stepping in to arbitrate. He shrugged and decided not to smack Itsuki after all.

"Fujimiya, how were your grades? Must be good, looking at your face."

"Well, I think I did fairly well," Amane nodded. "How about you?"

"Thanks to your help, I feel like I scored more points than usual," Yuuta said. "Though I won't know until I compare answers with someone later."

"I see; that's good to hear."

Amane had been worried about everyone's results, since their Saturday study session had turned into a video game tournament halfway through, but based on the impression he was getting from Yuuta, it had worked out okay.

Amane's expression softened a little as he thought back on that day and mused that it might be nice to get together and study like that sometimes. Itsuki's face then showed a clear look of discontent.

"Hey, you're letting Yuuta off awfully easy, aren't you, Amane?"

"Don't worry about him; reflect on your own bad habits."

"I believe that I am loved, even when you say such things."

"Don't get creepy. I—"

"That's right, there's only one person in this world who Amane loves."

Even though he muttered it under his breath, Itsuki had still crossed a line. Amane grabbed his friend in a solid headlock.

Yuuta laughed and made no attempt to interfere, as though he knew that Itsuki deserved it.

Chitose also seemed amused. "Itsuki, you're a real dummy." She smirked.

Itsuki, who was getting a knuckle forcibly ground into his forehead, had a foolish smile on his face, as if it didn't hurt at all.

Amane wasn't putting any real strength behind the attack, so it shouldn't have hurt that much, but he couldn't help but feel a little annoyed at how calm Itsuki was acting.

"Well, you're definitely devoted, Fujimiya. That's easy to see."

"Not you too, Kadowaki..."

"Hey, I didn't say what you're devoted to, just that you're devoted!" Yuuta beamed.

Amane couldn't think of anything to say, so he just turned away.

His behavior must have been amusing, because Itsuki, Chitose, and Yuuta all laughed like something was hilarious. Amane stared in the opposite direction, biting his lip and feeling extremely embarrassed.

Mahiru must have gotten free just at that moment. She locked eyes with him and smiled.

Amane groaned, feeling even more embarrassed now that Mahiru had looked at him, but she calmly walked over, wearing a smile on her face.

"Looks like you're having fun over here," she said. "What were you talking about?"

"Hmm? We were talking about how cute Amane is!"

"Watch it, Chitose—"

"That is what we were talking about, right?"

"Basically, they were all teasing me."

"Oh yeah, that too."

"See?! She admits it."

Amane shot Chitose a pointed look to tell her to cut it out, but Chitose seemed totally indifferent. Instead, he glared at Itsuki, who was supposed to be in charge of controlling her.

"Why are you glaring at me?"

"Maybe because you're the one who started all this in the first place?"

"So…what were you talking about, then?" Mahiru asked again.

"Oh, just the fact that Amane's a pure, innocent, devoted boy…," Chitose murmured. Amane really wished she would shut up already.

"I don't know what all this nonsense about being 'pure' or whatever is." He scowled. "What do you even mean, anyway? What's so pure about me?"

Itsuki put on a dramatic expression of exaggerated surprise. "Oh, don't tell me you weren't aware…?"

Amane kicked his friend under the desk and glanced over at Mahiru. She was looking upward slightly, with her usual smile on, as if she was pondering something.

"Actually, we were talking about how Fujimiya is rather stoic. I guess calling him straightforward would be more accurate," Yuuta added.

"I see." Mahiru nodded. "Fujimiya is definitely the type to work hard once he sets his mind to something. In that sense, he's a very straightforward person, isn't he? I think that's a wonderful quality to have."

"It really is. I just wish that he would have some more confidence about it."

"That's very true," she agreed.

Amane couldn't stand being there a second longer listening to the two of them mock him with their excessive praise.

He made eye contact with Mahiru, who gave him a gentle smile.

He felt embarrassed and immediately averted his eyes and saw that the rest of their classmates were looking over enviously.

Their attention was not focused on him, but on Mahiru and Yuuta, who somehow seemed to be hitting it off talking about Amane. That was a relief, but it brought up some slightly complicated feelings.

Seeing the two most popular people chattering away and getting along with each other would naturally attract attention. Amane felt a slight tinge of jealousy himself at the fact that neither of the two seemed to be the least bit bothered by everyone looking at them.

"What's wrong, Amane?" Chitose asked. "You're blushing…"

"I am not."

"You are too! And you're trying to hide it. Oh, Mahiru? After school, let's go have fun somewhere, all five of us. We're all together already, and the tests are over, so let's party!"

Completely ignoring Amane's uncooperative attitude, Chitose pivoted to Mahiru with a suggestion. It was a casual invitation, without too much pressure, but with her usual angelic smile still on her face, Mahiru answered, "Of course, if everyone wants to."

"*The five of us*" must have included Amane, too, but he probably didn't have the right to veto the plan, and Chitose must have understood that he wasn't likely to reject it anyway.

Chitose was wearing an expression that said, *"I got you!"*

Amane looked away again as he nodded his assent.

Chapter 8

A Reward from the Angel

"Hey, Amane, don't you think you tried *too* hard this time?" Itsuki grumbled, sounding somewhat astonished as he stared at the exam rankings that had been posted on the bulletin board in the hallway.

Even after their group study session, Amane had continued working diligently, preparing for the exams. He'd wanted to be proud of himself for a change. Also, the studying had helped distract him from certain coquettish words that had been whispered in his ear.

They were looking at the result of his efforts—and all the work he'd done to keep his mind off her suggestive expressions and the words that she had uttered—which had led him to rank sixth in their grade this time.

"Wow, it's hard to believe I made it that far."

"You really worked for it. Proud of yourself?"

"…Pretty proud, I guess. But there's no guarantee that I'll be able to do it again."

"What a stoic guy…"

He didn't want Mahiru to see him climb so high only to fall back down out of negligence. There would be no point to it unless he could consistently place in the upper ranks.

Considering that college entrance exams were also coming up, it would be absurd to be satisfied with this one success and give up trying.

Hasty preparations would not be enough for the entrance exams since students from other schools would also be vying for spots, so Amane vowed to keep studying hard so that he would be ready for what was to come as well.

Incidentally, Mahiru had placed far ahead of anyone else, in the top spot again. This was nothing if not expected, but Amane knew that it was because of how hard she worked, and that she never took it for granted.

"It looks like you took sixth place this time, Fujimiya."

Mahiru, who had arrived to look at the bulletin board after Amane and Itsuki, smiled beautifully as she noticed Amane's name.

She was in angel mode, and Amane smiled casually back at her, trying not to let any of his inner turmoil show on his face.

He felt the prickle of people's eyes on him, but he was already getting used to talking with Mahiru in public. The stares still made him uncomfortable, but he was able to soldier through without too much distress.

"Looks that way." Amane nodded. "Good for me, I guess."

"Heh-heh, he really worked hard, ya know," Itsuki interjected. "Studying during breaks and everything."

"...Ah, well—"

"If you worked that hard, shouldn't you give yourself a reward?" Mahiru asked.

"I...guess so."

Recalling the reward that Mahiru had promised him caused Amane to experience an indescribable surge of emotion.

She had promised to let him lie in her lap and to clean his ears. He had done so much to erase the thought from his mind that he had genuinely forgotten about it, but she'd said she would do it if he made it into the top ten.

He could always decline, but...there was no way he could bring himself to reject such an opportunity, if the girl he liked wanted to pamper him like that.

"...Speaking of which, congratulations on the top spot. Shouldn't you be the one treating yourself?"

"I suppose so. But it's not good to pamper oneself too much."

"But you're already so strict with yourself that I think you could stand to be a little indulgent. Well, that's not for me to say, though."

Now that they were on the subject, Amane realized that he would be receiving something special from Mahiru, but he had nothing to give back, and he wondered what he should do.

On the other hand, he had no idea what he could offer her, so he would have to ask about it after they got home.

Looking at Mahiru wearing her angelic smile, Itsuki quietly whispered to Amane, "How about you reward her?"

Amane didn't need to be told twice, and he made a mental note to ask her about it when they got home.

"Huh? A reward for me?"

When Amane posed the question to Mahiru as she was preparing dinner at home with her apron on, she turned around with a puzzled expression on her face.

Amane hadn't been able to settle down, remembering the devilish smile she'd put on the other day and thinking about the reward that was probably waiting for him after dinner. But Mahiru hadn't seemed to notice, and now her expression showed that his question was entirely unexpected.

"There's not really anything specific that I want, but..."

"Or something you want me to do...?"

"You do for me? Hmm, let me think. I guess I'd like you to cut that cucumber thinly with the slicer."

"That's not what I mean... Well, if there isn't anything, you don't have to force yourself to answer, you know."

Amane had a feeling she wasn't taking his question seriously, but he didn't want to push too hard, so he backed down easily.

If Mahiru really didn't need anything, that was fine, but if there was something she'd like him to do, and it was within Amane's capabilities, he intended to grant her request.

For the time being, she'd said she wanted him to feed the cucumber into the slicer, so he washed his hands and cut it thinly, but this was just helping her out rather than a reward.

"Rub some salt on that and set it aside."

"Yes, ma'am... Is there really nothing more?"

"Not really. I'm content with how things are at the moment... And anyway, I think that I'll be able to fulfill my one wish by myself."

"The wish you really want granted?"

"What do you think that is?"

Amane looked up from the slicer and saw Mahiru smiling gently.

For a second, her expression looked like the devilish grin she had worn the other day, and he couldn't bear to look directly at her, so he dropped his eyes back down to the countertop.

"...I d-don't know."

"Exactly. So don't worry about it. I'm happy as is."

Amane could sense the smile in her voice.

Mahiru went back to cooking, giving off an air like she wasn't going to let Amane investigate any further. Amane didn't know what to do, so he just kept on thinly slicing the cucumber.

"All right, lie down, Amane."

After dinner was over, the dreaded reward time arrived.

As if it was the most natural thing in the world, Mahiru sat down on one side of the sofa and smiled at him as she patted her knees. Amane was at a loss for words.

Mahiru's outfit for the day was shorts with black tights, so he would technically be lying in her clothed lap, but only an incredibly thin layer of fabric separated him from her skin.

To make matters worse, she had taken a bath after getting home today, and her whole body smelled wonderful.

It would be suicide for Amane to lie in her lap in such a risky situation.

"...No, um—"

"You don't have to if you don't want to, but isn't this what you asked for?"

"I-it is what I wished for, but the thing is, now that it's actually happening, I'm nervous, like...i-it's embarrassing, you know?"

"Well then, why did you ask for it?"

"Th-that must have been male instincts or something."

"Well, you can follow those male instincts, it's fine, but...this is your reward for working so hard. You don't need to be shy, okay? I'm going to spoil you a lot."

Mahiru patted her lap again, and Amane gulped.

It had gotten quite warm lately, so her tights were thinner than before.

He could just barely see the color of her skin through the sheer material, and it stirred up some strong emotions.

Even if her thighs were covered by the tights, the smooth beauty of her slender legs was on display, luring Amane in.

It probably wasn't Mahiru's intention at all, but the way she was dressed that day was going to be the death of him.

Rightfully, he should have somehow found a way to decline her offer and devise a peaceful way out for his heart and soul, but under the pretext of a reward, Amane's "male instincts" had gotten him into this mess.

Gingerly, he sat down beside Mahiru and lowered his head onto her lap.

He had experienced this once before, and just as he remembered, her legs were very soft. Since the fabric separating him from her was even thinner than it had been last time, the texture and warmth of her skin came through clearly, and Amane felt his heart squeeze tightly.

He wasn't sure where to look, so he faced upward for the time being and saw Mahiru smiling down at him.

His view of her face, however, was partially obscured by something...or, rather, two somethings. It was only May, but the temperature had been rising, and the shirt that Mahiru was wearing was also quite thin. On top of that, the material followed the lines of her body closely, highlighting her shapely figure beneath the fine cloth.

Amane had to turn over. If he stayed like that, he was going to explode from shame.

"All right, I'm going to clean your ears now."

Completely unaware of Amane's inner distress, Mahiru announced this with a smile. She sounded somewhat excited. Mahiru reached for the ear pick and tissues that were sitting on the table, and something soft pressed down on the side of his head.

(?!)

Sirens blared in Amane's mind, but Mahiru didn't seem to notice. She quickly grabbed the ear pick and sat back up. Amane's heart was pounding as he felt the weight of her soft body. Mentally, he was no longer prepared to handle an ear cleaning.

"Now, hold still," Mahiru whispered in a soothing voice, and she gently fixed his head in place with one hand.

She reminded him not to move while she was cleaning his ears, but Amane found it very difficult to stay still, for several reasons.

Even so, there was no way that he was going to struggle against her, so he stayed obediently still and stared hard at the side of the table as something rigid was slowly inserted into his ear hole.

He got chills for a moment. He was more sensitive where his skin was thinner. Amane never felt ticklish when he cleaned his own ears, but when Mahiru was doing it, he got a strange feeling, probably because he wasn't in control...and because it was exciting to know that it was the girl he loved who was doing it.

He knew that Mahiru was going to do a careful job because of her personality, but somehow having her oh-so-gently clean out his ear was kind of ticklish.

It was a little too tingly to really be pleasant, but at the same time, it had an unusual appeal that ignited certain desires.

At the very least, there was an indescribable niceness to it, pleasant enough that he was not going to resist having his ears cleaned like this.

"It doesn't hurt, does it?" Mahiru asked.

"Mm...it doesn't hurt. It feels good."

"Oh really? I'm glad. I've heard that this is supposed to be romantic for guys, but...well, does this feel romantic for you?"

"...A little, I guess."

"Well, you are a guy, after all."

"Have I given you any reason to doubt it?"

If Amane wasn't a guy, he wouldn't be writhing in agony on the inside, and he wouldn't be so excited by the softness of her skin. As it was, he couldn't help getting flustered being held close and pampered by the person he loved.

"Heh-heh, it's because you're such a gentleman, Amane. I didn't think you had much interest."

"On the assumption that I am a gentleman, what I want and what I do are very different. You ought to be careful; there are men who will smile to your face, then attack you when you're alone."

"By that logic, you wouldn't really be a man then, would you?"

Amane felt like he had just been called out and bit his lip unhappily. That said, it didn't seem like Mahiru had meant it as an insult. She continued peacefully with her cleaning.

"Here, Amane, turn over. I want to do the other side."

Even as he frowned harder, Amane turned and presented the opposite ear. Facing her belly, however, was a new kind of penance. If he looked down, he would see her shorts, and that wouldn't be good, so he had no option but to stare docilely at her stomach.

Amane wasn't sure if this was heaven or hell.

It would probably be heavenly if he could be honest about his desires, but as long as he was stuck between what he wanted and what he knew was right, it was like he was plunging one foot right into hell.

"...Amane, you've been kind of trembling since we started, but..."

"Please don't pay any attention to that."

There was no way he could even begin to tell her what he was feeling inside. After all, if he said any of it out loud, Mahiru would definitely pull away from him.

So there was nothing to be done but obediently accept the ear cleaning and hide his desires at all costs. This angel, pampering him innocently with no ulterior motives, was a frightening creature.

Mahiru seemed to have some questions about Amane's behavior, but he was facing her and couldn't make eye contact, so she gave up on investigating further and went back to cleaning his ear.

Feeling an inexpressible pleasantness and a ticklish sensation, Amane closed his eyes and waited for it to be over.

Whenever he opened his eyes, he felt slightly guilty about what was happening, so he kept them shut. But without his vision, his other senses seemed to become more acute. He inhaled her sweet smell, as well as the scents of her shampoo and body wash, and he felt the softness of her thighs. He was beside himself.

He couldn't stop thinking about how amazing it would be if he could have his fill of these sensations without holding back.

"Amane, when I'm done with your ears, can I play with your hair?"

"...If you want."

If he escaped soon, he wouldn't have to experience this conflict any longer. However, Amane was still a guy, and if a girl was going to let him continue lying in her lap, he wasn't going to argue. Even as he felt conflicted over wanting her to stop and wanting her to do more, in the end, he gave in to his desires. It made him realize that in many ways, he was very weak willed.

Mahiru gave every indication of being pleased by Amane's consent.

"I'm almost finished, okay?" she said as she carefully scraped out his ear.

Ah, over already? Amane thought, feeling just a little bit disappointed, suffering lonely agony yet again.

But he didn't let it show on his face or in his movements.

The slightly ticklish yet pleasant feeling came to an end as Mahiru pulled out the ear cleaning tool.

In its place came a different lovely sensation as Mahiru's fingers slipped smoothly through his hair.

"All right, all done."

Mahiru combed through his hair with gentle hands as if she was comforting a child, and Amane simultaneously felt embarrassed and like he wanted to surrender himself to her entirely.

He knew that if it came down to it, the latter feeling was stronger, and a silent groan threatened to escape his lips.

Mahiru's intention had been to pamper him thoroughly as a reward, and he was definitely getting spoiled.

Part of him wanted to fight against Mahiru, who seemed to be enjoying her chance to indulge Amane just as she had promised. Though it felt so good that any willpower he had was uprooted entirely, leaving him utterly helpless to resist.

...I'm getting spoiled...

He was getting his head caressed by her tender hands while fully savoring her feminine scent and warmth. It didn't sound like such a big deal when he put it into words, but it felt incredibly good and left him practically euphoric. Amane could imagine losing himself if he were allowed to enjoy these kinds of pleasures every day. The thought had a certain appeal to it.

When Amane let out a sigh and relaxed his muscles, he heard a quiet giggle.

"You're like a pampered little boy, for once," Mahiru softly teased.

"...Whose fault is that?"

"My fault." Mahiru giggled sweetly and swept her fingers through his hair again. "I always want to dote on you, because I want an excuse to touch you. Your hair feels so nice to brush."

"...Really?"

"Yes. It's smooth and glossy. How do you get your hair to do that...?"

"...I just use the shampoo my mom recommended."

Shihoko had been very insistent about making sure he didn't neglect and damage his fine hair. Subsequently, Amane used shampoo and conditioner found in beauty salons, the kind that boasted about being good for your lustrous locks. He didn't hate the scent of it, and he liked the feeling when he ran his fingers through his hair after it dried, so he kept using the product.

"You should talk, your hair is super smooth, Mahiru."

He gathered a tuft of the flaxen strands into his hand, and it felt even softer and smoother than his.

Of course, the girl had silkier, glossier hair; Amane's couldn't compete. Mahiru's had a texture that made him want to touch it forever, and it had a clean, soapy scent that wasn't overly strong. It was irresistible.

"I think this every time I pat your head, but you must take a lot of care in looking after your hair."

"…Well, I've never been negligent about it."

"I can tell. By the way, I've been touching your head whenever I like, but…is that all right? They say that a woman's hair is her life, and all that."

"…I like it when you touch me, Amane."

Amane was glad that she couldn't see his face, because he was sure his expression contorted into something strange when Mahiru said those words.

Shame, delight, confusion, panic… If Mahiru had seen all those strong emotions written on his face, she probably would have started to distrust him.

I get carried away because she says things like that.

Unable to say anything out loud, Amane tried to return to his normal expression. He closed his eyes and sighed.

When he opened his eyes, Mahiru's shirt was right in front of him.

Apparently, he had fallen asleep again—his consciousness had drifted away on a cushion of comfort and joy. Though he had no idea how long he'd slept, and that made him anxious.

The hand combing his hair had stopped.

He sat up timidly and saw that Mahiru was leaning back against the sofa, breathing heavily in her sleep.

"Defenseless," Amane mumbled at Mahiru, whose gentle breaths

©Hanekoto

were rhythmically rising and falling, then checked the clock and felt his cheek twitch.

It was an hour before midnight. He had been lying in Mahiru's lap since nine, after they had finished cleaning up dinner and doing other household chores. Which meant that he had been in the same position for almost two hours straight.

Mahiru had probably fallen asleep after being stuck on the couch for so long. Amane knew that she wouldn't have been able to bring herself to move and disturb him, so she had just nodded off where she sat.

He thought she ought to be more vigilant, since she was in a guy's apartment, but he was the one who'd fallen asleep in her lap in the first place, so he bore some responsibility.

He gazed at Mahiru's sleeping face, wondering what he should do, and decided for the time being to go ahead and take a bath.

Mahiru had already taken hers for the evening, but Amane hadn't taken his yet. Even if he was going to wake her up, it was better to let her sleep for now and get his bath out of the way. There was also the possibility that Mahiru would wake up on her own while he was bathing.

With that decided, Amane hurriedly went back to his room to get a change of clothes.

Once Amane finished his bath, he checked the living room and sighed softly.

As before, Mahiru was completely submerged in the depths of sleep and hadn't stirred, even with the noise from the hair dryer.

"Mahiru, wake up," Amane said, and gently shook her the shoulder. She was still fast asleep. Her head slumped to the side, showing she was truly unconscious, so for the time being, Amane propped her back up.

He figured it must have been tiring, sitting there with his head in her lap for so long, and she had probably nodded off. For now, it was clear that she wouldn't wake up any time soon.

I feel like this happened last time, too...

It must have been around the end of last year. He remembered lending Mahiru his own bed after she inadvertently fell asleep.

Amane had a feeling they were headed down the same path this time as well.

He shook her again, more forcefully, and called her name, but she didn't wake up.

He heard a quiet, little groan, but it was more like a snore than words.

This wasn't the first time that Amane had seen Mahiru asleep and defenseless, and he couldn't help but wonder, again, whether it was all right for her to have this much faith in him.

Cursing his luck, Amane poked Mahiru's cheek, but she didn't stir. He was only met with the feeling of her smooth and soft skin. His thumb traced a path down her cheek, stroking it gently.

When he reached her slightly slack lips, he found the texture to be even softer and more supple. They reminded him of ripe fruit and looked like they would taste sweet.

It wouldn't have been impossible for him to taste that sweetness in that moment, when she was this vulnerable. He could have enjoyed that delicious fruit and savored it as he pleased.

But Amane's self-control, and the knowledge that he would never recover if Mahiru rejected him, kept him back. Yet he couldn't stop touching her altogether. Amane laughed at himself for being such a coward, and he stared at Mahiru, whose beautiful sleeping face was so generously exposed.

She doesn't even know how I feel...

Mahiru probably had no idea how anxious he got when she was overly careless like this.

Unconsciously, Amane let out a huge sigh, gently stroked Mahiru's defenseless, sleeping face, and chuckled quietly.

Amane felt like he was being a shameful wimp, even more than usual. On the other hand, he was also convinced that his cowardice was what had allowed him to win Mahiru's trust.

It occurred to him that if he had gained her trust to this degree, he might be on the way to getting her to like him.

Even if he wanted to confess his feelings, he was too much of a weakling, too anxious about opening up to her.

"...If I could simply tell you I love you, I wouldn't have any worries," he grumbled quietly.

With the pad of his thumb, Amane gently stroked her tender lips and sighed.

The fact that the girl he loved trusted him this much and was here in this vulnerable state felt gratifying and lovely, but it was also torture. Before long, he was going to have to get her to understand the conflict he was feeling.

He made up his mind to scold her a little bit when she woke up, then grabbed her by the shoulders and shook her.

"Mahiru, wake up. It's time to go home."

He shook her kind of hard, to prompt her to wake up.

He could have stared at her adorable sleeping face forever, but if he looked too long, he was going to want to do something, and he wouldn't be able to sleep with her here anyway.

He had reluctantly allowed her to stay over several times before, or maybe it would be more accurate to say he had lent her his bed. He knew that, as a last resort, he could let her sleep in his room.

If possible, he wanted her to return to her own apartment. If

Mahiru slept in Amane's bed, it would smell extremely sweet and nice, and that would cause him all sorts of difficulties until her scent faded, and he wanted to avoid that if he could.

With that one goal, Amane shook Mahiru and gently slapped her soft cheeks. With extremely sluggish movements, she raised her eyelids with a flutter of her long eyelashes.

However, the vibrant caramel-colored eyes that peeked out from behind them seemed somewhat vacant and unfocused. He couldn't tell where she was looking, and her bleary eyes started to slip listlessly back behind the curtain of her eyelids.

"Mahiru, I'm begging you, please wake up. Go sleep at home."

"...Unh..."

"Don't groan, just say yes."

"...Yes..."

She answered him in a mumbling voice that didn't sound like she understood the situation, so with his cheek twitching, Amane tried even harder to rouse her back to consciousness, shaking her harder but not so hard as to rattle her brain.

It must have had some effect, because Mahiru showed him her eyes again, but—this time, she fell forward, directly against Amane, and buried her face in his chest.

In a quiet, muffled voice, she mumbled, "Smells nice," as she rubbed her cheek against him. A small sound squeaked out from the back of Amane's throat when he heard her moaning.

Seriously, this girl is...

He tried to tear himself away from her slack body, so defenseless that he had to wonder if she wasn't doing it on purpose at this point, but he couldn't. At the same time, he felt the urge to stay just as he was, to wrap his arms around her and dote on her. It probably would have been best to immediately pull away and go bang his head on the wall.

Biting his lip hard, Amane grabbed Mahiru's shoulders and

slowly pushed her away from his body, and she looked up at him blankly, with dazed, spiritless eyes.

"Mahiru, it's late already; how about you go home? We've got school tomorrow, you know, so if you oversleep, you'll have a hard time. I'll walk you to your door."

Mahiru only lived next door, but she was definitely out of it, so he felt anxious about her leaving the apartment.

Whether Mahiru had understood him or not, she said, "Good niii..." in a lifeless voice and staggered to her feet, which was a good sign. She looked like she might fall right back down on the floor, so Amane ended up rushing over to support her.

She was wiped out from the tests, and on top of that, she had let him lie in her lap for a long time. Sitting still for so long must have been physically taxing. Sleepiness was bearing down on her, and she could hardly stand.

...No way around it.

Amane was sure that even if he lent her his shoulder and somehow got her as far as her door, she would still fall flat on her face the second she walked in.

He sighed softly and gazed into Mahiru's face as she leaned her full weight on him.

"Mahiru, you've reached your limit, so I'm going to take you to your room. Can I borrow your keys? I'm going with you into your apartment."

He felt nervous about going into a girl's apartment and didn't like having to ask Mahiru for permission when she was obviously passed out. However, he figured that if she had to choose between that and staying over in a boy's apartment, she would probably prefer the former, no matter how many times she had done the latter already. Amane also knew he would be able to relax and sleep better if Mahiru was at home tucked into her own bed, instead of his.

He had roused Mahiru enough to ask for her permission, which slightly eased his discomfort.

In response to his question, Mahiru slowly nodded her head.

After confirming her consent, Amane pulled the keys out of Mahiru's pocket, trying his best not to make contact with her hip while he did so, and cradled her in his arms.

Mahiru must have been very tired, because she leaned into him and fell half asleep again. If Amane didn't get her back home soon, she was going to fall asleep right in his arms.

He stepped out of his apartment, trying his best not to make much noise. He walked over to Mahiru's door and, still holding her, carefully unlocked it. Then he slowly carried her into the apartment.

"...Pardon the intrusion."

The interior was, of course, laid out the same way as his. Amane knew it had the same floor plan, so he also knew where the bedroom ought to be.

But his heart started pounding the second he stepped in. Mahiru's apartment had a sweet, invigorating smell, and it was decorated differently from his. Her meticulous and tidy personality was evident. The flooring was polished to a high shine, and he couldn't spot any dirt worth mentioning. There was a mirror and some flowers sitting on the shoe cubby that stood against the wall, which gave the place a subdued, yet bright and brilliant atmosphere.

Amane glanced into the living room beyond the entryway. He got the impression that an adult had decorated it, with a collection of clean and cheerful furniture in basic tones of soft white and pale blue to go with the natural colors of the wood floor.

Despite that, the apartment didn't really look like anyone lived in it. It showed hardly any signs of habitation. Besides sleeping and going to school, Mahiru had recently been spending most of her time over at Amane's apartment, so in a certain sense, it was almost like she wasn't living there.

After having that realization, Amane quietly opened the door to the room he assumed was her bedroom and stepped inside.

It was the first time in his life that he had been inside a girl's bedroom. It was such a lovely space that Amane thought other girls would get upset if they had to live up to this standard.

Just like the living room, the basic colors were white and light blue, but it was fancier than the living room. He would best describe it as tidy and stylish.

Amane also thought that it looked more lived-in and showcased Mahiru's personality more. The place was well-kept, as was Mahiru's habit. On top of the desk, next to her textbooks and cookbooks, sat the stuffed animal that she had won at the game center when Amane had taken her there.

Also, the stuffed bear that he had gifted her for her last birthday was there, just as immaculate as on the day he'd given it. It was sitting beside her pillow on the bed, and it now had a navy-blue ribbon tied inconspicuously around it, mostly concealed by the original ribbon that had always been there.

Amane had heard that she treasured the stuffed bear, but seeing in person that she had it sitting there by her pillow, he felt his cheeks grow hot.

Imagining her sleeping with it every night was almost too much to stand.

Biting the inside of his cheek in a desperate attempt to keep it together, Amane slowly lowered Mahiru onto the bed and covered her with the blanket. He was once again grateful that she had worn shorts with tights today.

Maybe because she felt the sensation of her body sinking into the bed, Mahiru, who had been almost entirely asleep, opened her bleary eyes a little.

Smiling in spite of himself at her sleepy expression, Amane got down on his knees and gently stroked Mahiru's head with the palm of his hand.

"You're home now. I'll give your key back later, so don't worry about that."

She had touched him plenty that day, so he figured it would be all right to touch her a little bit, too. As he scooped up a piece of hair that had fallen across her face to move it out of the way, he poked at her supple cheek, and she giggled like it tickled and put on a smile that was several times softer than usual.

Without pause, with sleepy, bleary eyes, she patted the bed beside her.

"...You too, Amane..."

He froze as he considered what the rest of that sentence could mean.

She seemed to be telling him to sleep there. Maybe even that she wanted him as a body pillow.

...She doesn't mean that; she doesn't know what she's saying.

Amane tried to persuade himself of this as he pushed back against certain desires that had momentarily threatened to lure him astray.

He was afraid that if he lingered, Mahiru would say something unthinkable, so he impatiently stroked her head very gently, like he was putting a child to bed, and lulled her to sleep.

"I'm going home now. Okay?"

"...No."

"There's no way I'm hanging around in a girl's bedroom. You'll absolutely regret asking once you wake up. I can already see you beating me with your pillow."

If Amane joined her in bed, not only would he be unable to get

©Hanekoto

a wink of sleep, but once she woke up, Mahiru would be confused and would turn bright red. Then, to hide her embarrassment, she was almost guaranteed to whack him with her pillow.

He could also anticipate that afterward, things would get awkward between them, so for the sake of Amane's sanity and the next day's mood, he had to use all his willpower to get out of there.

Mahiru was still dozing off, but seemed to be resisting sleep and Amane's frantic attempts to pacify her.

In that case—Amane grabbed the bear from beside her and pushed it against her face.

"This guy says he'll sleep here instead of me, so relax and go to bed."

It appeared she had been keeping the stuffed animal close when she slept, so Amane decided to use it to lull her to sleep.

He untangled his fingers from her soft hair and gently, gently whispered good night. Mahiru groaned in an adorable voice and embraced the stuffed bear in front of her.

She looked innocent and childlike, a far cry from her usual prim and proper act, and so sweet that he wanted to caress her again.

She was so charming that he might have spontaneously snapped a picture, if he'd had his smartphone on hand, and he felt relieved that he hadn't brought anything with him other than the key to his apartment. It would be very inappropriate to photograph a sleeping girl's face. He knew it was weird to even consider it.

At last, Mahiru's eyelids, rimmed with long eyelashes, covered the entirety of her eyeballs, and she started breathing peacefully in her sleep.

Amane sighed quietly, careful not to wake her again.

...She's too careless. That was terrifying.

Amane knew that she only behaved this way because she was with him. That didn't change the fact that it was difficult for him to watch the girl he loved let her guard down so completely like that.

Praising himself for resisting temptation, Amane left Mahiru's room as silently as he could and walked right out of her apartment.

He knew that it would take quite a bit of time before he was able to sleep that night.

"G-good morning..."

"M-morning..."

Inevitably, the next day, the two of them each felt too awkward to look at the other. Mahiru almost never came to his apartment this early, but naturally, given what had happened, she had come over to talk.

Amane had had difficulty falling asleep after everything that had happened yesterday, and it didn't make it any easier when she suddenly appeared first thing in the morning.

He recalled the pleasant sensation of lying in her lap, the rich fruity scent, and the full softness that had come down on his head in the middle of it. Then the memory of Mahiru's apartment, which he had basically entered on his own, with permission at least, surfaced in his mind. Her cherubic sleeping face and sweet pleading voice were impossible to forget.

He had spent the night tossing and turning in bed, tortured by how lovely she had looked while hugging the teddy bear.

Writhing in agony, he had just finally managed to go to sleep when morning arrived, but he was awakened by his alarm, resulting in his current state of exhaustion.

Mahiru, on the other hand, looked fresh and had a good complexion, as if she had slept just fine. She seemed very anxious, though, and constantly fidgeted like she was trying hard to conceal her embarrassment.

Amane had been just about to eat breakfast when Mahiru had barged in. Now he was stuck, unsure of how to proceed.

Her reward had been too exhilarating, and now that he knew that feeling, he found it hard to look at Mahiru directly. To make matters worse, Mahiru didn't seem to realize what had happened, so feelings of guilt weighed on his chest, in addition to the shame.

"...Wh-what are you doing here in the morning? Oh, I know, you came to get your key back, right? Sorry for taking it home with me."

"Ah, no, I...well, there is that, but that's not why I'm here."

No matter how close they might be, Amane felt it was wrong to take home a girl's house key. He was already feeling bad about setting foot in her apartment, even though he hadn't really been able to avoid it.

...As I suspected, she's mad that I saw her bedroom.

Amane remembered her room being very neat and tidy, but he couldn't fault her for being upset that he had rudely taken a look while she was basically unconscious. If he'd happened to see her underwear or something hung up to dry, Mahiru probably wouldn't have looked at him or spoken to him for a while, and Amane was sure he would have had to avoid her for some time as well.

Thankfully he hadn't caught sight of anything like that.

"C-can I ask you one thing?" Mahiru inquired.

"Sure."

"...O-on top of my desk, there should have been a picture frame, but..."

"A picture frame?" Amane asked.

It wouldn't have been polite to scrutinize her room too closely, so Amane had only taken a quick look around, and he didn't particularly remember there being one. It sounded like it had been jumbled in with the rest of the stuff on her desk, judging by her tone.

Amane searched his memory but had no recollection of a picture frame, so he figured he had just missed it.

"No, I didn't see one, but...did something happen? Did I bump into it and break it, or something?"

"N-no! A-as long as you didn't see it, that's fine...if you didn't see it."

Apparently, Mahiru had something displayed in a picture frame that he wasn't supposed to see. Her obvious relief made him kind of wish he had. But it was a matter of privacy, so he wasn't going to say that out loud.

Mahiru looked like a great weight had been lifted from her shoulders.

Amane scratched his cheek. "I tried not to look at your room too much, you know? All I saw was the lineup of stuffed animals I gave you, and the teddy bear by your pillow that you sleep with..."

"Forget you saw that!" Mahiru slapped Amane's arm softly.

"But you already told me about it...," Amane answered without thinking.

Mahiru glared at him. "Don't tell me I was hugging the stuffed animal while you were there."

"...You were half asleep, and you demanded that I sleep there with you, which I wasn't about to do, so instead, I brought you the bear to sleep with."

"Sleep there with me?!"

Mahiru looked shocked, like she couldn't believe her own words. Gradually, her whole face turned red.

She must not want to believe she said something like that when she was half asleep...

"D-did I really say something like that?!"

"N-not only did you say it, you actually called my name and patted the space beside you...like you were telling me to climb into the same bed..."

©Hanekoto

"Aaugh!"

Mahiru put her hands on her cheeks and made a pathetic noise. Her face was bright red, and her eyes were wavering like she might cry.

"N-no way, I don't usually have such...thoughts! I just, um, I... felt relaxed since you were around, so...it's not that I really had any untoward desires...it must have been something like I wanted your b-body heat, that's it."

"What's that supposed to mean?"

"Please don't ask me anymore!"

It was truly rare for Mahiru to raise her voice, and she was breathing hard as she sharply turned away.

For once, Amane was the calm one. "F-fine, I don't really understand why you're so upset, but I'm not going to pry. Just be careful from now on. You were half asleep, but I did more or less get your permission before I took you home. But if you hadn't woken up, I was going to have to put you to bed in my room."

"...That would have been fine."

"What did you say?"

"Nothing."

Amane could tell that she had said something quietly, but he hadn't been able to make out Mahiru's mumbling. It seemed like it wasn't meant for him to hear.

"Anyway, you've got to understand that no matter how much of a trusted friend I am, I can't just let you sleep here. If you try it again, I'll have no choice but to use you as a body pillow when I sleep, no joke."

Though he had just made quite a bold claim, Amane knew that he wouldn't get any rest if something like that happened. He was just trying to warn Mahiru against being so careless. There were a few people she really trusted, but he still thought she ought to be more cautious, even around those companions.

In response to Amane's slightly critical tone, Mahiru blinked dramatically, then put on a faint smile.

"Says the same Amane who fell asleep so easily in my lap. You've dozed off in my lap twice now, you know?"

"Th-that's a different conversation. It's a completely different matter for a guy to fall asleep in front of a member of the opposite sex than for a girl to do it. I wouldn't be in any danger."

"...Even though you don't know for sure that I won't do anything?"

"Would you?"

"Let me think... Maybe I would take your picture or something, as a joke."

Amane grew weak as Mahiru looked at him smugly, as if to say, *"What do you think about that?"* but Mahiru didn't seem to notice.

"...I wouldn't really care, but now I'm going to have to check your phone."

"And what if I saved it on the cloud before you realized, and then deleted it from my phone?

"Stop talking about it. I'm starting to believe you might try and it's freaking me out. Also, my 'doing something' and your 'doing something' are different matters, so seriously, be more careful." Amane grabbed her shoulders and spoke soberly. "You're not understanding me at all."

Mahiru looked surprised, but didn't pull away, and didn't avert her eyes, either. "I understand perfectly well. It's fine."

"You really don't. Not even a little."

"How rude! I said I do. I think you're underestimating me."

"If you understood, you wouldn't be doing these things."

"...You still need work, Amane."

Amane frowned, not sure why she was getting so frustrated with him, but Mahiru just sighed softly, slipped out of his grasp, and headed for the hallway.

In Mahiru's hand was the house key that she had come to collect, which she must have grabbed without him noticing. He had left it on the tray on top of his shoe cubby in the entryway of his apartment.

"You have some thinking to do, Amane," she said as she left his apartment.

Amane thought that she might just as well direct that line at herself. Holding his forehead, he grumbled, "Which one of us doesn't understand?"

Chapter 9

The Angel's New Clothes

Exams were over, and it was the middle of May.

The sun's gentle rays grew brighter as it created a springlike atmosphere. It was that time of the year when it was starting to get uncomfortable to wear long sleeves.

May was supposed to be the time for a seasonal change of clothing, but the work of pulling out his short-sleeved shirts and summer slacks was awfully troublesome, and Amane had been putting it off.

Though the air conditioners in school were set to the perfect temperature, as soon as he took a single step outside the classroom, or set off to and from school, he felt hot. Eventually, Amane came to the decision that it was time to get his summer clothes out.

"It's getting to be the season when we'll want short sleeves, huh?" Mahiru asked. She'd nodded in understanding as she watched him pull his summer clothes out of a garment case that he stored in the back of his closet and threw them into the washing machine to wear for tomorrow.

Incidentally, Mahiru was also still dressing in long sleeves and tights, in a way that avoided exposing any unnecessary skin.

She had switched to wearing a sweater vest under her blazer, but looking at her all covered up, Amane worried that she might be hot.

"The weather is changing, and I've been feeling a little sweaty. I'm thinking it's about time for me to phase out my long sleeves, too. Today was really warm, wasn't it?"

"You never let your clothes get sloppy, eh, Mahiru? You button everything up properly, and don't roll your sleeves up, and you usually have tights on…"

"People always stare at me when I let any skin show, and it really bothers me. I feel compelled to dress that way… It's like a form of self-defense."

Mahiru was beautiful and had a very keen sense of style, so she was often troubled by people's gawking.

No matter what, she attracted attention, and that often included inappropriate stares. Amane wasn't unsympathetic to the fact that men were naturally inclined to look at beautiful women, but he could tell that Mahiru hated to be ogled.

"I'm never sure how to dress for summer," she said. "Last year, I wore some really thin black stockings, but they were still pretty warm."

"Seems like they would be. Girls have to wear more pieces of clothing than guys do, which seems like it would be hot…"

"Well, I can put up with a little warmth if I'm doing it to protect myself, but…the issue of overheating is a real problem."

Mahiru sighed and said she hated summer for that reason. Amane didn't know how he should answer and ended up staying silent. Mahiru didn't seem to mind, and let her gaze wander over to the washing machine.

"So you'll start wearing your summer clothes tomorrow?" she asked.

"Well, I was thinking it's about time to change. It's already this sweltering…"

"I see. I've also been considering it, but before I can go to school,

I feel like I've got to try everything on at least once to check the fit. I think my size hasn't changed, but just in case..."

Mahiru seemed very concerned about maintaining her figure, and it didn't seem like she would have let herself get out of shape.

Amane admired her strong willpower and discipline. He knew that he could never be as strict with himself as Mahiru was with herself, but he wished that he too had an ideal body that he could maintain. First, he would have to start by getting his ideal body, though.

"I'd better try mine on, too, or it could be bad. I've gotten a little taller since starting school, so if they don't fit, I'll have to buy new ones at the school store."

Amane had purchased his summer uniform before starting high school, so now that he was in his second year, he was worried it might be a little short on him. It had been fine during the summer of his first year, and he hadn't had any problems with his winter uniform, but his clothes might have become a little bit too tight for him, even though he'd initially bought them a bit larger.

He had grown more than five centimeters since starting high school, and there was a good chance his summer clothes were too small.

Thinking he would try them on after the laundry was finished, Amane gazed over at the washing machine, which was making a dull mechanical noise.

Mahiru looked up at him.

"...You're pretty tall, aren't you, Amane?"

"Well, I guess I'm a little taller than average."

Amane was about one head taller than Mahiru, who was still staring up at him.

Mahiru had a petite build, but that didn't mean she was particularly small; in fact, she was average. Amane's eyeline was just a little higher than it had been when he had first met her, which made him realize again that he had been growing.

Usually, he stood at a bit of a distance when talking to Mahiru, so as not to overtax her neck, but recently, she had been standing much closer to him, enough to touch, and he'd started to worry about her neck getting cramps.

Mahiru didn't seem to care about such things at the moment. She was scrutinizing Amane and frowning slightly.

"...I do worry about you, though. You don't weigh very much, for how tall you are."

"That's why I'm exercising and training to put on more muscle," he replied. "More importantly, why do you know how much I weigh, anyway?"

"Because I saw you weigh yourself on the scale by the sink when you woke up late one weekend. I was the one who pushed you over to the sink, when you were half asleep."

There was nothing Amane could say to that, so he stayed quiet, but Mahiru looked at him with exasperation in her eyes.

"It looks like you're working hard, and I see you putting in the effort, but you've got to eat a little more after you exercise, Amane. You're thin, and it makes me worry. After all, food is what builds the body, right? If you tell me ahead of time when you're going to exercise, I can adjust the menu."

"I'm really making a lot of work for you, but...I'm grateful for the offer. And since we're still on the topic, you're kind of thin yourself. Sometimes I worry you might break, so you should eat more, too, please."

Of course, Amane was grateful; he never had to worry about meals thanks to Mahiru. She was even gracious enough to prepare extra food to help with his weight training.

But he thought that Mahiru herself ought to eat more, too. He could tell she was delicate even through her clothes, and occasionally when he touched her, she was so thin that he was anxious he might break her. From what he had seen, she had never been one to eat that much, which probably made it easier for her to manage her figure, but it concerned him that she was so petite.

"You're super thin," he said, and grabbed her narrow waist, realizing just how lean her body really was.

A high-pitched shriek came from Mahiru's mouth, and the sound interrupted any further thoughts.

"...Ah, s-sorry," he fumbled.

"N-no, it's fine, it's okay," Mahiru said. "Just, if you touch a girl's belly too much...there are girls who develop complexes about that stuff, okay?"

"I'm really sorry for touching you like that. It's sexual harassment to touch a girl's body without asking, isn't it? I'm very, very sorry."

"Okay, you don't have to go that far..."

Although they were good friends, they were still the opposite sex, so naturally, Amane was very careful about how he touched Mahiru.

But he had just touched her stomach—not her head, or her hand, or her shoulder, but her stomach, a very personal location. He had gotten worked up about how thin she was, but that was no excuse, and he immediately regretted touching her belly without her permission.

"I don't really mind it that much, so calm down, Amane. And anyway, I don't suppose you do things like that with anyone other than me?"

"I don't have this kind of back-and-forth with anyone other than you," he answered. "Also, I hardly ever interact with any other girls. It's not like I would randomly touch a girl I don't know that well."

The only other girl he might possibly touch would be Chitose. She was slim, a bit like Mahiru, but it was more of a lean athleticism, different from Mahiru's petite delicacy. Though he would never even really touch Chitose like that in the first place, aside from occasionally, playfully bopping her on the head.

"Well, I'm glad to hear that," Mahiru nodded. She seemed satisfied with Amane's answer. Then, maybe as payback, she leaned forward and pressed her palm against Amane's stomach, touching him through his shirt.

He wasn't going to scold her, considering he had just done the same to her, but it tickled, and he felt embarrassed about his body.

Compared to how he had been before Mahiru had improved his diet, he was healthier now, but his body was still a far cry from his ideal muscular figure.

It had been quite a shock to hear that she was worried about him being too thin, so he knew he needed to eat and exercise more to build muscle onto his frame.

"...Do you think I'd be better if I were a little stronger, Mahiru?"

"Strong is nice, but I think that at the end of the day, the most attractive type of body, for either sex, is a healthy body. Also, this is my personal opinion as a girl, and I would absolutely never want to force it on anyone else, but...when a girl is standing next to a really skinny guy, there's a possibility that she will feel awkward, so maybe a medium build is better than being all skin and bones."

"I see..."

"B-but you're not necessarily...I wouldn't go so far as to say you're too thin, okay, Amane? But it would be healthier for you to eat a little more. You're not the type to overeat, despite being a high school boy. Speaking of which, Amane, um, when it comes to girls...do you like slim ones best?"

"It's rude to comment on girls' physiques," Amane answered immediately. It was something he thought every guy was supposed to know.

Both his parents always told him, *"If you say something, and it goes over poorly, prepare to see blood,"* so Amane always avoided commenting on anybody's figure.

"Ah…" Mahiru sounded like she understood his flat assertion, and her gaze drifted off into the distance. He figured that girls must have the same understanding.

"Well, I guess it's better to be on the slim side," Amane said. "But if you're too thin, it's worrisome, because it can be bad for your health and might mean you're not getting enough nutrients. It gives peace of mind to see that someone has the proper amount of muscle and fat on them."

"…That sounds more like something a parent would say than something you'd hear from a young man, don't you think?"

"You're one to talk."

"Fair enough, but…"

If anything, Mahiru was the one who had a motherly attitude sometimes. So Amane didn't think she had any right to accuse him of having a "parental" gaze or whatever.

"Even if I'm not worried about you, I don't think there's any need for you to be on a diet, Mahiru."

"Really?"

"Where could you possibly lose it from? You've got your ideal body, and now you're trying to maintain it, right? It's not my place to say anything, but I think the best body for you is one you feel confident about. And personally, I would worry if you got too thin, so I'd like you to stay just as you are."

He would definitely be concerned if Mahiru, who was already quite thin, lost any more weight. He wanted her to know that her figure was fine just as it was. If she wanted to get any skinnier, he would have to stop her.

"I understand that it's difficult to maintain a certain figure, but I think it's more important to be healthy."

"...Sure."

Almost in rhythm with Mahiru's nodding head, the washing machine continued tumbling his laundry around with a loud rattle.

"Good morning."

The following morning, when Amane woke up, Mahiru was there in his apartment.

He turned around and looked behind him at the clock in his bedroom. It was time to get up and ready for the day, not time to leave his apartment yet.

Mahiru had visited his apartment a handful of times in the morning before, but it was something that generally didn't happen, so Amane's sleepy mind was confused.

"...Morning?"

Mahiru had a spare key, and he had told her she could come in as she pleased, but he hadn't expected to encounter her so early in the day.

When, in his bewilderment, he returned her greeting with a questioning tone, Mahiru put on a gentle smile.

"I know it might be rude for me to come over like this in the morning, but...I was hoping I could get you to check something for me before I left home."

"Check something?"

At that point, he took a second look at Mahiru and realized that he could see a bit more skin than usual.

"I changed my clothes. Does anything look off?"

"Ah, summer clothes...uhh, no, well—"

"Yes?"

"...I'm not sure having your legs bare...is a good idea."

Summer clothes meant short sleeves, but that wasn't what Amane was talking about. When he looked down, he could see her pure, pale thighs peeking out from under her skirt.

School uniforms featured longer skirts than most street clothes, and Mahiru usually wore tights as well, so he hadn't gotten a good look at her bare legs before. In keeping with school rules, Mahiru's new skirt was plenty long enough to keep everything covered, but even so, her bare legs were now exposed to the air.

Amane was understandably flustered, and his eyes darted around nervously.

"Well, I was thinking that not many girls wear tights at school right now," Mahiru said.

"That's true, b-but I don't think it's right for y-you. It's no good."

"Is that because you can't handle seeing my bare legs?"

"Th-that's not it!" he protested. "It's more like, if you show them off, the other boys will probably make a fuss and stare, so it's a bad idea, I think."

The day before, they'd had a whole conversation about Mahiru's black stockings. Amane had never thought she would appear without them.

The pale expanse of her legs was too dazzling. He couldn't look right at them.

"You sure you're not going to stare, too, Amane?"

"Everything has a limit, you know!"

"But it's a fact that you saw my legs when I twisted my ankle, remember?"

"That was an emergency, and anyway, I was a perfect gentleman! I even covered your lap with my blazer, didn't I?!"

Sure, he might have caught a peek at her legs when he'd knelt down beside her, but he'd been careful to drape his blazer over her so that he couldn't see anything untoward. He'd devoted all of his attention to treating her ankle so that he wouldn't look anywhere inappropriate. Hence, he had honestly never ogled Mahiru's legs. Even Amane knew better than that.

"Well, are you having any imprudent thoughts right now?"

"...No."

"The way you hesitated is a bit worrying."

"No!"

"Don't get all worked up. Sorry for teasing you too much. I've known from the start that you weren't looking at me like that. You just don't know where you should be directing your attention."

"If you knew that, then you shouldn't have felt the need to question me..."

"No, it was necessary for my own satisfaction. Making your heart pound is the most important part, you see."

"So you did this just to give me a heart attack?"

Clearly, Mahiru had wanted to start the day with a bit of fun.

Amane looked at her grudgingly as he realized that he'd fallen for it, hook, line, and sinker. Mahiru, the prankster, just stared back at him, grinning in her elegant way.

"Relax," she said. "I brought stockings with me, and I was planning to put them on."

"Unbelievable..." Amane groaned, knowing she was trying to get a rise out of him. Then he decided to get a little bit of revenge and stared back into Mahiru's caramel-colored eyes that were twinkling happily.

"...So you don't mind me looking at you?"

"Huh?"

Mahiru stared at him in surprise.

Without breaking eye contact, Amane continued, "You went out of your way to come show me your bare legs. That must mean you want me to look at them, right?"

"...That's, um, I don't really mind...if you see them—"

"You don't think it's a big deal..."

Mahiru seemed very confused. "That's not—it's not necessarily the case, though..."

Amane sighed softly. "Well then, don't show me. You should only do things like that for people you want to look at you."

He wished she would put herself in his shoes and imagine what it was like for a guy to see a new side of a girl he loved. But of course, he couldn't say anything like that. It was only the start of the day, and already he was feeling exhausted.

Timidly, Mahiru tugged at the sleeve of Amane's pajamas. "...Wh-what if I said I came to show you because I wanted to?"

Her quiet voice trembled bashfully as she looked up at him with watery eyes. This time, Amane completely froze up.

"Because I wanted to see your reaction... But all you said was that it's no good," Mahiru mumbled, looking a little dejected.

Amane shook his head frantically. "Th-that's because it's not. Look, how do I say this? It's troublesome, like...I don't know where I'm supposed to be looking..."

"So you think bare legs don't suit me?"

Amane reluctantly looked down at Mahiru's outfit. She was dressed in a crisp, ironed short-sleeved blouse and skirt. The outfit exuded her usual tidy elegance, while also giving off a fresher image, and the buttons and ribbon on her shirt, done properly all the way up to her neck, were a reminder of her serious nature.

Amane might have preferred it if it were a little harder to see all the angles and curves of her figure, but these were her summer clothes, so there was nothing to be done about it.

He looked her over once, trying as best he could not to let his eyes linger on her perfect, slender legs, then slowly opened his mouth to speak, a little fraught.

"...You look very cute, and those clothes suit you, so please, go put on your stockings immediately."

"Okay."

Mahiru must have been satisfied by these brief, carefully chosen words of praise because she gave Amane a gentle, broad smile and nodded.

Momentarily struck speechless by that smile, Amane turned away before Mahiru could notice, looking toward the bathroom sink.

"Don't come playing tricks on me like this again. I'm going to wash my face and change, so while I do that, please sort your clothes out and get ready to leave," he said, speaking somewhat more quickly than usual, and hurried into the bathroom.

Mahiru giggled softly behind his back.

Amane finished getting dressed for the day, and when he headed into the living room, Mahiru was sitting quietly on the sofa waiting for him. She was fully covered, in black stockings and a sweater vest. Amane wondered if what he'd seen earlier had even been real.

He couldn't help but feel exhausted by the whole affair.

"...You know, if you'd shown me this look from the start, I would have been able to offer you an honest opinion, without worrying about how my heart is going to hold up."

"How nice for you; you got a special treat."

Mahiru grinned shamelessly, which made him a little angry. He walked up to her and pinched her cheek, but she still kept smiling happily.

"...Well then, I'm going to leave for school ahead of you," Mahiru said, standing up from her seat after watching Amane devour the breakfast she'd prepared.

To get him back in a good mood, she had made a rolled omelet.

Amane was fully aware of her ploy, but couldn't help feeling better anyway and went with her to the door to see her off.

They walked the same route to the same school, so it seemed a little ridiculous to leave separately. Even so, there was no way they could arrive at school together, thus the only other option was to stagger when they left.

"See you at school," Amane said. He was planning to wait long enough to avoid suspicion, as always, but he noticed that Mahiru was wearing a somewhat dissatisfied expression. He tilted his head questioningly. "What is it?"

"...Just wondering if there will ever come a day when we can walk together."

"The stares alone would kill me."

Recently, Amane had been seen interacting with Mahiru more and more often, and their classmates seemed to have gotten used to it, to a certain degree. However, Amane still received many jealous looks, and when it came to the students in other classrooms, they often glared at him.

Amane was already fed up with being on the receiving end of their overly aggressive stares, and if he and Mahiru started going to and from school together, the negative attention was sure to increase to a level he had never yet experienced.

"I suppose that's to be expected," Mahiru sighed. "...Though we're just reaping what we've sown, at this point. It's all so exhaustingly inconvenient."

"I imagine that having everyone at school make a big deal of you just walking with a guy would be pretty unbearable for you, too, no?"

"Actually, I don't really care if anyone makes a big deal out of it, but I know it would cause trouble for you. If it didn't bother you, I'd be more than happy to go together."

"...You're sure about that?"

"If our timing matches up, that is. It's a pain to go out of our way to stagger the times we leave, and it's inefficient on days like this. Besides, isn't it more fun to walk to school with someone you like?"

"That's true, but—"

"Isn't it? I guess reality doesn't always go the way we want it to."

After a big, exhausted yawn, Mahiru shook her head once and then transformed before his eyes, putting on her usual elegant, angelic smile.

"All right, I'm off. I wanted to show you my new summer look first thing in the morning, so I'm glad I was able to come do that," Mahiru said casually. She batted her eyes at Amane, who was still frozen in place by her provocative statement.

"See you later," she said as she opened the front door. "Make sure not to be late, okay, Amane?"

Mahiru slipped bashfully past the doorway and set off for school. Amane leaned his head against the wall of the hallway for a little while, then decided he should go wash his face again. He was seriously worried about what was to come.

Amane left his apartment late enough to give Mahiru a solid head start. When he finally arrived at school, he was not surprised to see people gathered around her, checking out her new outfit.

The temperature had been steadily rising, and it was definitely time for new clothes to match the season. Plenty of students had already changed into short sleeves.

Even though Mahiru was wearing lighter summer clothing, she looked very prim and proper in it. Though because of her gorgeous appearance, her change of outfit still attracted more attention than usual.

On top of all that, Chitose had gotten to her seat and declared, "That hairstyle looks like it's sooo warm!" and tied Mahiru's hair up in a ponytail for her. The unusual hairstyle was drawing even more stares—with her hair up, the nape of Mahiru's neck was visible.

Amane didn't like that much. Mahiru was obviously free to style her hair any way she wished, but he couldn't help but feel upset that other people were staring at the girl he loved.

...How can I think that way? She doesn't belong to me.

Amane glanced over at Mahiru again, practically seething with unwarranted jealousy. He was starting to hate himself for it.

Itsuki peered at Amane with that strangely perceptive look of his. "Oh, are we feeling a little out of sorts?" he asked slyly.

Amane brushed him off with feigned ignorance. "...Must be your imagination."

Then for some reason, Itsuki looked over at Mahiru and nodded like he understood everything.

When he looked back at Amane, he was smiling, or rather grinning. Amane could feel himself getting even more flustered.

Chapter 10

The Angel's Gaze and Amane's Struggle

"Amane, pass it here!"

"But you've got terrible control!"

The school Sports Day was coming up next month, and the students were leisurely enjoying gym class.

Remembering the previous Sports Day, Amane knew once the teams were announced sometime next week, the whole school would start preparing for it, but for now, they were still having regular gym classes.

Listening to the echo of the basketball club's squeaking shoes, Amane glared at Itsuki, who had thrown the ball sloppily into the wall as a joke, and chased after the ball as it rolled away.

They were playing basketball that day, and soon it would be time to practice their shots. It sounded like they were going to have a game during the second half of class. Amane wasn't particularly good at basketball, but he didn't mind tossing the ball into the hoop a bit.

As Amane chased the old, brown basketball rolling slowly away from the wall, he shot a quick glance across the net dividing the gym in two. On the other side, the girls' class was playing badminton. The girls were supposed to have been outside, but due to a sudden downpour, everyone was having gym inside the divided gymnasium.

The girls also seemed to be playing leisurely, and from time to time, Amane would catch sight of one of them lightly batting the shuttlecock with their racket. He grabbed the ball and jogged back.

He was careful not to even look in Mahiru's direction. He wanted to avoid any chance of anybody noticing and accusing him of having a crush on the angel.

He did like her, but he knew it would be troubling for her to hear those sorts of rumors. He also didn't want to let any unfamiliar classmates know about it, so he kept it a secret.

"Stop throwing the ball off in weird directions," Amane said. "It'll be awkward if I have to go get it from the girls' side."

Itsuki grinned foolishly. "Come on, don't be so sensitive."

Amane threw the ball with a little force at his friend's stomach, and Itsuki, who wasn't particularly bad at sports, caught it without breaking his grin. With a long sigh, Amane got a new ball from the ball hamper.

The members of the sports clubs were always in high spirits during these sorts of gym classes. This time, it was the basketball club that was in their element, and they were especially lively.

Amane didn't really like basketball, but he was surprisingly fond of shooting practice, so he had been throwing the ball at the basket all class, to show the gym teacher that he was taking it seriously.

He threw another ball. It arced through the air, rebounded off the backboard, and fell through the center of the basket. Amane retrieved it with a slight feeling of satisfaction.

"You're good at this kind of thing," Itsuki observed. "Though whenever a game starts up, you lose all your motivation, and then you're useless. You should try harder."

"Be quiet. You can't expect someone who's a natural-born introverted member of the 'go-home club' to put in a ton of effort in a basketball game. Obviously, the guys in the sports clubs are going to be the ones actually playing."

"I guess so. Hey, I was just thinking, you ought to show that special someone how cool you can be from time to time."

Amane knew exactly who Itsuki was referring to, but he wasn't going to just nod obediently.

"I don't need you to worry about that," he said. "She already knows that I'm no good at sports and that I'm very uncool."

"Why do you always have to turn it around like that?"

"You have to know by now that telling me to make an effort here is a losing proposition, right?"

Amane looked at Itsuki, who seemed disinterested in the outcome, with a sour expression, and was confronted with more cackling laughter.

"Come on now, this is your chance," Itsuki urged.

"It is not. Why don't you give it a try then, see how it goes?"

"Huh? No way, man. I'm not that good."

"Well then, where do you get off telling me what to do?"

Amane grabbed Itsuki under the chin and squeezed his cheeks with his fingers, warning him not to casually demand things that he couldn't do himself.

"Sorry, sorry!" As he was laughing it off, Itsuki looked over to the other side of the net. "But she is looking over here, though."

"Huh?"

Amane followed Itsuki's gaze and saw Mahiru, waiting her turn to play badminton, looking in his direction. Staring, to be more accurate. She was definitely staring at Amane.

She was probably just killing time by looking around, but Amane suddenly started feeling uncomfortable, now that he knew he was being watched. He pursed his lips awkwardly.

Itsuki mumbled, "Better try your best," like he was glad it wasn't his problem, and pulled Amane along with him after the gym teacher's whistle sounded.

For the practice game in the second half, the class was divided into two teams, to play against two different teams from another class.

Amane and Itsuki were playing in the second round, so to avoid getting in the way of the rest of the players, they climbed up onto the stage at the end of the gym and took a seat.

The two of them were watching the imposing figure of Yuuta, who was on the team playing the first game. He was putting on a good show.

"How is Kadowaki keeping up against the actual basketball club...?"

Some of the players on the opposing team were in the basketball club, but Yuuta played well enough to put them on equal footing. Even though Yuuta was an experienced athlete, at the end of the day, he could not match them point for point. If it had just been a matter of speed, the track star might have had an advantage, but when it came to agility and handling, not to mention the coordination required to shoot the ball, the members of the basketball club were able to show off their specialized skills.

Amane had expected the basketball club would have an advantage and that his classmates would be entirely shut out, but Yuuta quickly disproved that prediction by continuing to score points.

"Well, Yuuta's the product of an athletic family, after all," Itsuki said. "He just chose the track club because he likes running, but he can play just about any sport at a high level."

"How is he so strong?"

"Apparently, his mother was a sports trainer or something like that. I think he told me that his older sisters are going into related occupations, too."

"So he's the result of a gifted education."

"Whoa! Watch Kadowaki, guys!"

"Block him, block him!"

"Don't let him get anywhere!"

"Are we sure he doesn't have some awful grudge against us?"

"If he finds a good opening, this is really gonna look bad for the basketball club!"

Amane was half-listening to the cries of the opposing team. He could also hear the girls cheering Yuuta on from across the partition.

They seemed to have started their own tournament of badminton on the other side of the gym, and the girls who weren't actively playing had come up to the net to watch the game.

The other boys, as well, were understandably enthusiastic about Yuuta's performance. Murmurs of admiration swept the crowd. For some reason, Itsuki slapped Amane on the back.

In the end, their class was victorious in the first game. Amane jumped down from the stage, marveling at his amazing friend.

Throwing on the team jersey he had been given, Amane stepped onto the court, not bothering to hide his expression of irritation, and accidentally made eye contact with Mahiru on the other side of the net.

She was wearing a faint smile, different from her usual gentle, angelic type. It was Mahiru's real smile, the mellow one that she always showed him at home.

There was a tenderness to her gaze, as she waved her hand slightly and slowly mouthed *"Do your best!"* at him.

She didn't say it out loud, but Amane imagined he could hear it, and it was too much for him. He couldn't stand to look at her and turned away.

His mistake was turning to face Itsuki.

"Feeling fired up now?"

©Hanekoto

"Shut up," Amane snapped back desperately. He felt completely transparent when he heard Itsuki laughing in an apparent effort to break the tension.

"...I'm gonna die..." Amane groaned, squatting down to catch his breath. He was playing basketball seriously for the first time in a long time and pouring all his energy into it.

His heart was pounding violently.

Even though he had recently started to exercise a little more, he hadn't yet fully exerted himself like this and hadn't ever done such a strenuous workout. Coupled with the match, Amane was extremely exhausted.

Amane coughed and slowly tried to get his breath back, but his heart was pounding away and showed no signs of calming down.

During the match, he had accidentally taken a dramatic fall, so his battered body ached and his breathing was ragged. He was having a really hard time.

Even though he had tried not to overdo it, clearly, he'd gotten carried away.

I feel like I looked really pathetic out there.

He'd fallen right in front of Mahiru. He felt depressed thinking about seeing her afterward in the classroom. Far from showing her how cool he could be, the only thing he'd shown off was how much of a loser he was.

"Amaneee, you okay?" Itsuki asked, crouching down next to his friend to take a look at him. He must have seen Amane squatting off to the side while the teams shook hands.

"...I'm fine, but I'm definitely gonna be sore tomorrow."

"Ha-ha, that's because you got a late start on exercising!"

Amane felt a quiet gratitude toward Itsuki, who was rubbing his sore back even as he teased him. He took several deep breaths, and his heart started to calm down.

His body was burning hot, and it hurt where he had hit the floor, but Amane didn't regret playing this hard. He figured that pushing himself from time to time was a good thing, even if it wasn't in his nature.

Amane sucked in one more big breath and decided to go cool off for a bit.

After gym class was over, Amane changed clothes and washed his face in the locker room.

Lunch period was next, and everyone else headed out as soon as they finished changing, complaining about being hungry, so Amane was left with a moment of silence.

He had planned to meet Itsuki and the others in the cafeteria, but he felt awkward about facing Mahiru at the moment, so he spent a long time trying to cool his face off with the water. He may have gotten carried away, soaking himself all the way up to his hair, but he was all damp with sweat anyway, and that was probably exactly what he needed to rinse it away.

I can't believe I fell right in front of her.

Of all the places he could have fallen, he had done it dramatically, right where Mahiru was standing—he remembered her expression when it happened.

Amane was scowling when he heard quiet footsteps approach from behind.

"Are you all right?"

It was a familiar voice, but one he would rather not have heard now. Amane slowly stopped splashing his face and looked up.

He didn't want her to see his pitiful expression, so he bit his lip and took a deep breath. Somehow resisting the urge to run away in shame, Amane combed back his wet, clinging hair and turned around.

"What's wrong?" he asked, pretending to be calm. "You're still hanging around here? Not eating lunch?"

He could see that for some reason, Mahiru seemed agitated.

"Oh, no, it's just...you fell, so I was worried if you were okay... Akazawa told me you were here, so—"

"That Itsuki... You really don't need to worry; I just banged myself up a little bit, that's all."

Mahiru was avoiding making eye contact as she spoke to him, and Amane got the feeling that her angel mask was about to peel off, though he wasn't sure why. It was perplexing.

She had appeared upset when he'd taken his fall in front of her, but this seemed to be a different sort of agitation.

He tilted his head quizzically. "Shiina?"

"...No, it's nothing, so don't worry about it. Also, Fujimiya, that sort of behavior is against the rules, so please don't do it again."

"What are you talking about?"

"Anyway, it's not allowed."

Once in a while, Mahiru would say something that Amane just didn't understand, and this time, he was especially puzzled. Mahiru cleared her throat without answering his question, pulled herself together, and stared straight at Amane.

"...Earlier, you were protecting us, weren't you?"

"You just happened to be standing there, that's all. I would have taken the hit even if it hadn't been you that was there."

Earlier, in gym class, the girls had been poking their heads through the net that roughly divided the gymnasium, so that they could better cheer on the boys. A stray ball had flown perilously close to where the girls had been standing.

Amane had only fallen because he had just barely managed to block the ball that was flying toward the opening in the net.

Be that as it may, he wanted absolutely no thanks for it, and he would have been grateful, though bruised, if she had just let it go.

"It was nobody's fault but my own, so you can laugh at me if you want."

"That would be entirely impossible. I'm really grateful. But...that said, I wish you wouldn't do such rash things."

"I couldn't help it."

Amane looked away as he dried his face with a towel. When he finished, Mahiru was looking up at him with an exasperated expression.

"...You looked cool out there, but once we get home, let me take a good look at where you fell, okay Amane?"

She spoke in a quiet voice that only Amane, standing at this distance, could have heard. She sounded insistent, like she wasn't going to let him get away without an examination. In response, Amane averted his eyes without agreeing and grumbled, "I'll do no such thing."

Despite his attempts at protesting, when they got home, Mahiru forcibly removed his shirt to tend to his injuries.

After she was done, Amane realized that Mahiru had coerced him into getting half naked. He blushed bright red and wasn't able to make eye contact with her for a while.

Chapter 11

The Angel Drops a Bomb

Exams were returned and results announced, and Amane and the other second-year students reached a period of relative calm. Club activities resumed, and all they had to do was prepare for Sports Day, the next upcoming event, in about three weeks' time.

Some students, depending on their scores, had to take supplementary lessons, as well as supplementary exams for certain subjects. But Amane was in the clear, so during this brief period of calm, he spent his time taking it easy.

Talking with Yuuta after school, Amane got a strained smile from his friend when he brought the topic up.

"I don't actually have much down time, though," Yuuta said. "I've got club activities, and I have to practice for the interscholastic athletics competition."

Yuuta had already become known as the ace of the track and field club in his first year, and the coaches and managers had more expectations of him. He never failed to put in the effort to live up to those.

Yuuta had once called Amane "stoic," but from Amane's perspective, that word described Yuuta more than him. It was probably exactly that earnest effort that made him so popular and well-liked.

"Oh, that's right, it's still a ways off, but the chance to show off your accomplishments is coming up, huh?"

"Mmm. With the competitions approaching, I'm gonna need to shorten my times more, but I don't mind since I like to run anyway."

"Will you be all right? My image of the track club is that it's pretty demanding."

"Maybe it is, but it's not like the club is ancient Sparta or anything. The coach knows you can't get good results just by going all out every day. There's a balance to it: We rest during break times, and when it's time for club activities, we work hard."

"Huh...sounds like it's definitely an enthusiastic club."

"I think it does require discipline and motivation, but if it was one of those high-energy clubs with no time to rest, I probably would have quit already. If I'm just running, I can do that anywhere. That's probably why Shirakawa quit."

"...Oh yeah, she went to the same middle school as you and Itsuki, right?"

"Yeah, she did. Itsuki and Shirakawa are both so different now compared to back then, you'd probably be shocked."

Now that Yuuta mentioned it, Amane remembered hearing that Chitose's personality was quite different than it had been in middle school. He hadn't known any of them at that time, so it was difficult for him to imagine.

The only version of Itsuki and Chitose that he knew was the cheerful couple and constant life of the party.

Their past didn't seem like a topic that they liked to discuss much, so Amane hadn't probed deeply, but they must have changed considerably if it was enough for Yuuta to mention.

Amane was curious. But on the other hand, with an expression that said he was worried about upsetting Itsuki and Chitose by saying too much, Yuuta related gently, "I'm not going to talk about it, but maybe they'll tell you themselves sometime."

Amane had no intention of forcing the information out of him, so he nodded with understanding. Itsuki didn't butt into Amane's personal life, so Amane decided he wouldn't go sticking his fingers into his friends' pasts, either.

"Going back to the topic of track and field, getting too obsessed and running mindlessly only leads to injuring your muscles and tendons. For me, you know, running track is important, but it's not everything in life. So I'm pretty happy with the way the club does it."

His smile was so dazzling that Amane had to squint to look at him. Looking a little embarrassed, Yuuta made an awkward face.

"Well, that's enough about me, right?" he said. "Let's forget about club activities for now; we've got the day off."

"You're the one who brought it up."

"That's true, so all the more reason to put a pin in that. Come on, let's go home."

Amane laughed quietly at Yuuta, who was clearly trying to change the subject, and the two of them left the classroom.

Itsuki and Chitose happened to not have any supplemental lessons that day and had apparently left earlier to go on a date. It worked out that club activities were off for the day as well, so Amane wanted to seize the chance to hang out with Yuuta. While chatting casually after school for a bit, they'd decided to stop somewhere on the way back home.

As they walked down the hallway, Amane spotted a familiar flash of gold farther down the hall. He looked again, thinking to himself that it would be unusual for her to still be at school, and saw that for some reason, she was holding a large quantity of printouts in both arms.

"...What are you up to, Shiina?"

"Oh, Fujimiya and Kadowaki! It's unusual to see you still here at this time. Especially you, Fujimiya."

"I could say that right back at you... What's up with those?"

Amane pointed at the printouts that she was struggling to hold with both hands, and gave a small, wry smile.

"The teachers asked for students who had time to help staple together printouts for next month's Sports Day. I couldn't say no... they just gave them to me."

"...You don't feel like you're being exploited for free labor?"

For better or worse, the teachers depended on Mahiru as much as the other students. Amane had witnessed her getting constantly saddled with odd jobs, and this seemed like one of them.

Mahiru was a prodigy who did well in school and at sports, but she wasn't a member of any school clubs, so she was often given work from teachers who thought she had an abundance of free time. They probably knew she could never turn down a favor due to her kind nature.

"I do have time to spare, so...I'll be done with this pretty quickly. This is the last bunch that I'm taking to an empty classroom, and once I've carried it all over, I just have to staple them, and then I'm done."

"What does the school have secretaries for, then?"

"Well...it's fine. Despite what it looks like, I'll be done in a little over an hour."

"But you're talking about voluntarily giving up over an hour of your own time!"

Amane had some complicated feelings about Mahiru being a model student and getting exploited by the teachers in situations like this. But Mahiru either didn't mind or was just used to it, so Amane relaxed and gave her a weak smile.

"Anyway, that's why I wanted to let you know I'm going to be a little late getting home today, by about an hour or so. But the sun has been setting later, too, so I'll be fine." Mahiru said this like it was nothing, and Amane sighed softly.

"...Sorry, Kadowaki, could we push today's hangout to another day?"

"What a coincidence, I was just thinking that."

It seemed the two had been thinking the same thing.

Amane and Yuuta looked at each other and smiled, then casually grabbed the printouts from Mahiru's hands.

Mahiru must not have been expecting it. She blinked several times, stunned, and seemed to take a minute to understand what had happened. Then, she grabbed Amane's sleeve in a panic.

"F-Fujimiya, give those back!"

"Where are you taking them?" Amane asked.

"Umm, to an open classroom on the second floor...but that's not the point!" she insisted. "I was asked to do this."

"It's not like they have anything confidential written on them, since they gave them to a student," he said. "And anyway, they didn't say you couldn't have help, did they?"

"Th-that's true, but...say something, please, Kadowaki!"

"Ah-ha-ha! Fujimiya, you can't do that," Yuuta mock-scolded. "You have to let me carry half."

"Here ya go."

Smiling at Mahiru's grumpy look, Amane handed half of the papers to Kadowaki. Mahiru seemed to realize that it was pointless to protest any further.

Amane could feel her reproachful eyes on him but let her gaze slide right off as he headed for the classroom she had indicated.

"...I didn't mean to steal your time from you," Mahiru muttered.

"Nobody's stealing my time. I'm using it as I please."

Amane was doing it completely voluntarily. There was an argument to be made that he felt compelled to do her this favor, but it was better than Mahiru toiling away alone.

Yuuta was smiling calmly and seemed to agree, so she ultimately gave up on saying anything else. She glared at Amane with a tiny bit of resentment, which he pretended not to notice.

Despite it all, Mahiru didn't stop them. He figured she probably just didn't know how to respond to the favor.

"…You dummy."

She insulted him outright in an adorable way that he had never seen her do at school before. Both Amane and Yuuta burst into laughter.

Mahiru, whose angel mask had slipped off a little bit, narrowed her eyes as she walked beside the boys—

"So not only does she curry favor with the teachers, she's flirting with boys, too. All while telling us that she's got an 'important person' or whatever."

"Seriously. She's such a suck-up."

Amane heard voices from somewhere, and he felt his body stiffen as he walked. He glanced around but couldn't see any girls who might have been the voices' owners. He decided they were probably somewhere behind him.

Beside him, Yuuta's smile didn't change, but the look in his eyes was serious. Amane remembered him confessing once that he absolutely hated people who spread gossip, so it didn't seem like he would be able to forgive what they just heard.

Even Amane was on the verge of saying something, but he knew that would just make things worse, so he kept his mouth shut and peered over at Mahiru.

Mahiru didn't seem to think anything of it and had on her usual calm expression, as if she was accustomed to such treatment.

That expression made him uneasy, and without meaning to, he found himself staring at Mahiru. She must have noticed, because she put on a gentle smile and said, "Thank you ever so much for helping me. Let's finish this up before it gets too late, shall we?"

Her voice was calm and collected, and both Amane and Yuuta nodded, unable to say anything further.

The three of them worked in awkward silence, and once they had finished the job, Mahiru left for home first. After waiting a while to stagger their times, Amane headed back as well.

When he returned to his apartment, he took a long look at Mahiru's face.

Her expression was the same as always, and no sign of hurt or anger darkened her beautiful face. Instead, it was Amane who felt irritated as he recalled those girls' words.

Mahiru noticed the sour look on Amane's face, and she quickly gave him a bitter smile.

"Are you perhaps worrying about what happened at school earlier?"

"...It's bothering me."

Of course, he was going to get angry at people who wouldn't say anything to her face but snuck around in the shadows bad-mouthing her.

Amane sat down beside Mahiru and took another long look at her; she was smiling at his behavior like she always did.

"That kind of stuff doesn't bother me so much. I expect that degree of gossip, actually; it would be stranger not to hear it."

Amane was the only one who was bothered by it and by Mahiru's total, nonchalant acceptance of the idea that some people hated her.

He knew the reason why Mahiru conducted herself as an angel, so it was surprising that it didn't upset her, and his awkward expression showed it.

"I-is that really how it is?"

"It's only natural, right? It's not like everyone is going to like me, you know. It would be kind of scary if a person like that existed," Mahiru said quietly and dispassionately, twirling a piece of hair around her fingertip as if she was bored.

"I think that I make it easy for people to like me," she continued, "but I doubt that works for every single person in school. It's just that all the kind voices are usually louder and easier to hear. The supportive voices of kind people just help block out the hate. I mean, even you didn't like me that much at first, I think."

"...It truly pains me to hear you say that, but..."

Sure, before he had gotten to know Mahiru, when he had only known her by her reputation, Amane had thought of her as someone who excelled in everything and was beautiful. He knew that she was desirable due to those traits.

But he would say he fell into the category of people who didn't particularly care much for the angel, at least not on a personal level. When everything about her had seemed too perfect, he'd found her almost unapproachable.

"Especially among the girls," Mahiru said, "there are people who act friendly on the surface, when they actually hate me. Since so many people admire me, they bad-mouth me to mask their own insecurities. I just try to get along with as many people as I can. It makes everything easier, you see."

Mahiru matter-of-factly evaluated her position relative to the people who hated her. Amane wasn't sure what he could possibly say in response.

He figured that girls and boys must live in different worlds, with different rules for human interactions. If Mahiru was telling him this, it probably meant that there were people out there who shunned her, and she had really heard them say such things before.

He wasn't able to come up with the right words and couldn't do anything but sit there uneasily. Mahiru must have noticed, because she relaxed into a smile.

"There are way fewer of them now, but there have always been a certain percentage of people who hate me, so I'm used to it. I'm careful to conduct myself in a way that reduces that number as much as possible, but it will never be zero. There are some people who detest me because the majority likes me."

"...Isn't that painful?"

"Well, I'm sure I wouldn't like it very much if anyone ever said it to my face, but to date, no one has made such a declaration. Besides, I'm sure that people like the ones today who say they hate me aren't talking about the real me; they just resent my outward appearance and social standing. There's not really anything I can do about that, so I don't plan to try."

"That's very pragmatic..."

"If I wasn't pragmatic about it, I wouldn't be able to stand acting the way I do at school."

Mahiru, who was more disciplined than anyone Amane knew, had a quiet, thoughtful look in her eyes. A small sigh escaped her lips.

"I am aware that, objectively, I have more attractive features than many other people," she said. "Some of it is genetic, but I also put a lot of work into my appearance. There are people who find me superficial just because I value that."

Her words weren't an exaggeration or presumptuous in any way; they were the foundation for her self-confidence.

Certainly, Amane was not about to deny her natural beauty, especially having seen her mother, who she took after.

But Mahiru's charms didn't lie in the features she had inherited.

Her demeanor and conduct, the way she wielded her gaze and her expressions, the very atmosphere that surrounded her...she had not been born with any of those things, but they were what made her truly lovely. Amane thought that her remarkable intelligence and personal character were more beautiful than even her outward appearance.

...Still, she is very pretty...

Mahiru's willpower was so brilliant, it seemed like he would be burned by the radiance. Mahiru herself seemed like she also might be scorched by that light, and it was a little scary.

"I put a lot of effort into things you can't see on the surface, you know. That's why some people who can only see the end result assume that I must be cheating somehow. And their feelings of envy aren't my responsibility. Of course, if I was able to correct one thing, I think it would be the way people talk about me and Kadowaki. We get along well, but there's absolutely nothing romantic going on between us. People misunderstand that and get jealous, which is bothersome."

"I...I see..."

"I mean, have I ever behaved like I was into him? I think he's a considerate and likeable guy, but I don't have any romantic feelings toward him at all. But people start speculating if I so much as talk to him, and it's annoying."

What seemed to really bother her was the sheer frequency of the rumors.

Mahiru and Yuuta, who had been transformed into idols of sorts by their schoolmates, were often paired up in people's minds, since they were both role models to their respective sexes.

In reality, they barely interacted. When Mahiru had made Amane's acquaintance, she at best knew of Yuuta as a popular guy on campus but hadn't known him personally. They only became friends when Amane started hanging out with him.

Amane had never suspected that Mahiru had any romantic feelings toward Yuuta. She had always treated the "prince" of the school with impartiality.

"Maybe to the girls crushing on Kadowaki, it looks like he's already taken," Amane said. "Most guys, if you approached them, Mahiru, would go crazy for you."

"Hmm, it doesn't seem like you're in that group, Amane."

"...Well..."

He was already completely infatuated, no approach necessary. He felt like nothing she did would change how deep his feelings of love for her were, but he couldn't tell her that.

Amane glanced nervously about as he tried to come up with a response, but Mahiru was staring directly at him.

He couldn't stand the pressure, so he looked away from her, but he saw her sigh from out of the corner of his eye.

"At any rate, Kadowaki isn't my type. Objectively, he is very handsome, and quite the well-mannered gentleman, too, but...how do I put this...? In some ways, our situations are similar, so I'm happy to have him as an acquaintance or friend, maybe even as someone I can look to for support. But I don't feel like any of that is leading toward us falling in love."

"...I guess when you think about it, you and Kadowaki do have some things in common," Amane agreed. "Though there's not such a big difference between his public and private self as there is between yours."

This was something that Amane had come to understand recently as he'd gotten to know Yuuta better. Like her, Yuuta also tended to try to act the way that everybody expected him to. However, it wasn't as obvious as when Mahiru did it, and he usually let some of his real personality show through.

Mahiru had no choice but to act the way she did because of her family background. The reason she did it and the degree to which she had to maintain the act were different, so they were similar but not the same.

"You make it sound like I have a split personality... A-are my public and private selves really that different?"

"They are, but how can I put this... Your true self is much cuter than your angel persona. At first, well, you seemed cool and serious, but once I got to know you, I found you to be an honest person who's much shier than I expected. The way you express emotions with your words and actions is completely different, too, so...yeah, there's a difference, you know?"

"Wh-who exactly do you think is making me act like this?"

"...That's, well, hmm. It's not on purpose."

It wasn't that he was doing it intentionally. It was just that Mahiru got embarrassed easily whenever someone gave her an honest compliment.

Amane understood perfectly well that she had always been a hard worker and very disciplined, so he had been trying to give her frank, genuine praise as often as he could. If that brought out her bashful side, well, it was too late to do anything about that.

"I think it's even more wicked of you to do it not on purpose, though."

"You could say the same thing about yourself. You're the heartless one, Mahiru."

"What is that supposed to mean?"

"...In your case, you've been getting more and more touchy, and it's hard to deal with."

Mahiru especially had no room to criticize Amane. She had a talent for making people blush and used it quite often. To make matters worse, she often carried out surprise attacks, forcing Amane into difficult tests of willpower on a daily basis.

At the word "touchy," Mahiru's large eyes opened even wider, and she blinked several times. Then she gasped, and her lip started trembling.

Amane couldn't help but notice a deep red slowly staining her cheeks.

"I-it's not on purpose." Once she'd reached a lovely shade of cherry, Mahiru offered this excuse in a wavering voice. "There are times when I do touch you on purpose, but I never meant to make you uncomfortable."

"I have several questions about your definition of 'on purpose,' but I know that you didn't really mean anything by it. You should just be careful, though, because if a girl does stuff like that too often, someone could get the wrong idea."

"…I only do it with you."

"I know that, too. That's why I'm telling you."

Amane couldn't be certain what kind of feelings Mahiru had toward him, but he knew she thought he was special, and that she liked him.

Still, he was a guy, and her thoughtless contact often troubled him. He thought he'd appreciate it if she toned it down a little, for his sanity's sake if nothing else.

When he looked in Mahiru's direction, Amane noticed that her face was still very red. Mahiru smacked his upper arm playfully.

"See? That's what I'm talking about," he protested.

"That time was on purpose."

"Okay…"

Mahiru gave Amane a bit of a scowl. He didn't understand what he'd done wrong. Even though she was glaring at him, the expression on her face and the embarrassment in her eyes made her look nothing if not adorable.

Amane got the feeling that if he told her she looked more cute than scary, she'd probably be even angrier.

So, he didn't say anything at all, and Mahiru cleared her throat and straightened up.

"Anyway, back to what we were talking about earlier," she said. "It doesn't really bother me that some girls hate me. It's a childish dream to think that everyone will always get along, after all, and I know it'd only cause more problems trying to force it, so I've accepted that certain people just won't like me."

"...Mm-hmm."

"This contradicts what I was saying earlier, but after pretending to be nice and acting the part of the angel that everyone adores for so long, recently I've started to think that maybe I've had enough."

"Really?"

Amane never expected to hear those words from Mahiru, who maintained her angelic persona with such tireless consistency, and he thoughtlessly repeated her words back to her.

Mahiru smiled faintly. "I've been thinking, maybe I don't need to be such a good girl... I've always tried to keep up an act so that everyone will like me, even though I knew it wouldn't work on everyone. But if I had someone who could discover the real me, and really see me for who I am, I could be happy just being myself, I think."

Mahiru's eyes wavered with a certain lonesomeness as she thought back on her past self, and soon her caramel-colored eyes shone brightly.

"You said you wouldn't take your eyes off me, right, Amane?"

Anyone could have seen that the light contained joyful hope for the future. It wasn't sparklingly radiant, but gentle and kind, the sort that had real warmth and affection in it.

As she gave him a look filled with such brightness and emotion, Amane gulped loudly.

"...I made a promise, so..."

"Yes, you did."

Mahiru's face melted into a broad smile at Amane's affirmation. Her expression seemed dazzling and vibrant, different from the calm in her eyes, and he found that he couldn't look away from her.

As though from somewhere far away, Amane felt his heart pounding hard as he tried to sear the image of her smile into his memory.

"So that's why I don't have to get too worked up about anything. I'm not going to go out of my way to change how I act at school, and I'm not going to worry too much about it, either. It's all right, because I've got someone who sees me for who I am and accepts me."

"...I see."

Because Amane had discovered the real Mahiru who had been huddled up inside, and he was looking at her for who she was.

That was what let her stay calm.

Overwhelming feelings of joy and love welled up inside him, tickling his chest.

But a small lump also formed there, blocking that feeling just a little bit.

"...You look sort of dissatisfied, don't you?"

Mahiru had noticed that something was bothering Amane and turned to him with a troubled, anxious look on her face. He couldn't say for sure that it was dissatisfaction he was feeling, though.

"N-no, it makes me happy that you've started feeling that way. I think it's a great thing. But it's just, well, I've just...got some thoughts."

"What is it? Tell me now."

"Ah, no, it's—"

"I'm not going to get mad or anything! I can't even imagine you saying anything to hurt me."

The pressure of her eyes staring directly at him was enough to tell him he wouldn't have the chance to refuse.

After all, Amane had also said some things that could be misinterpreted, and knew he should explain himself, but—

He also believed that if he put what he was feeling into words, he might be setting himself up to be teased for his immature emotions.

"Fine. D-don't laugh, okay?"

There was no way that he was going to get out of telling her, so he tried to warn her first, and she nodded obediently. He found it unbearable to look at her directly, so Amane averted his eyes somewhat from Mahiru and opened his mouth to continue.

"Now, you said you wouldn't get worked up..."

"Right," she answered.

"The thing is, sometimes you let your guard down and show your real self without meaning to..." He made it that far, then hesitated to say any more, but it was too late to stop, so Amane took a deep breath. His lip quivered as he carried on. "...And when I think about another guy seeing you like that...I dunno, it makes me feel...conflicted."

He paused for a moment before reaching the conclusion of that thought, because he knew right away how childish he sounded.

He was glad that Mahiru had accepted herself and was starting to change the way she thought about things, and he was happy that she had extended a hand to him, after spending many years wearing the same protective shell.

He was also happy that she had placed her wholehearted trust in him.

And he was overjoyed that she seemed to be coming to feel that she could be herself, without keeping up false appearances.

He should have had no complaints, and yet he hated the idea of Mahiru—this completely ordinary, sensitive girl, who always worked hard despite difficult circumstances, who got lonely with surprising ease and was bad at depending on others because she tended to put on a show of courage—he hated the idea of all the other students at school getting to see that girl.

I know that it's just possessiveness and jealousy making me feel like this.

But that was what he truly felt, despite knowing that she didn't belong to him and that he had no right to feel the way he did.

"L-look, I know that this sounds presumptuous, and that you'll probably want to tell me off, but—"

Amane pursed his lips in self-derision, marveling at how shamefully pathetic he must be. Mahiru looked at him, blinking her round, cute eyes in surprise, clearly taken aback. Gradually, both corners of her lips started to curve upward.

By the time Amane noticed, she was already grinning, and her demeanor had changed to something warm and cheerful.

"I—I thought I told you not to laugh!"

"Heh-heh, sorry!"

When Mahiru apologized with a wide, defenseless, cherubic smile completely free of any ill will, it was all Amane could do to catch his breath. He couldn't offer any further complaints.

It was a different type from the one she'd been wearing before, an expression in her eyes of pure joy and affection that surpassed anything he had seen. It left Amane speechless.

Mahiru let her smile drop just a little bit and fixed her eyes on Amane again. "...You don't have to worry, Amane, I'm not going to show anyone else the kind of faces I show you. There's no way I would feel comfortable enough with people I'm not close with."

"I—I see."

Amane was understandably relieved and became keenly aware that his emotions were plainly visible on his face.

Usually, he was better at hiding his feelings, but when it came to Mahiru, no matter what he did, the things he tried to conceal showed up on the surface.

"...You're such a cutie, Amane," Mahiru said, while smiling like something was funny.

Amane bit the inside of his cheek and squeezed, keeping his facial muscles locked in place. "Stop that. You're making fun of me, aren't you?"

"I mean it," she insisted.

"That's uncalled for; quit it."

"You quit it, stop showing me such a cute side of you."

"I'm going to have to challenge that. I mean, what about me could possibly be considered cute? And why would you say that to a guy?"

As someone who prided himself on shedding all his adorable traits, Amane didn't have a clue what she meant.

Women and children could accept the word as a compliment, but Amane was a guy and had no desire to be cute, so he could only take it as simple teasing.

He frowned and protested with his eyes, but Mahiru let out a little giggle that told him her evaluation wasn't going to waver.

"Everything about you is endearing."

"I can't trust it when a girl says that, and I don't agree."

"What an awful thing to say. Well, you have to understand the fact that a girl's definition of cute isn't just based on appearances but is more a sign of whether she finds something likable in a broader sense… That's why you're definitely cute, Amane!"

"Guys aren't happy about being called that, you know."

He did not appreciate the girl he liked choosing this way to compliment him. Nonetheless, he was happy about the fact that she was praising him, but Amane would never call a guy like himself adorable.

He thought about asking her why she thought he'd be happy that she called him cute, but he got the feeling that she hadn't been trying to compliment him specifically so much as just to state her own opinion, so there didn't seem to be any point.

Amane pressed his lips together tightly and looked at Mahiru, but she was still smiling joyously. If he hadn't been able to see the affection in her eyes, he probably would have pinched her cheeks right then.

"...Is there nothing attractive about me?" Amane grumbled quietly, without meaning to.

Mahiru stiffened up and fixed her eyes on him, which made him immediately regret his words.

Even for a pitiful loser like Amane, begging for compliments was too much. Anyway, there was no chance that Mahiru thought of him as someone who was cool when he had been told by plenty of other people that he was a lazy, pathetic late bloomer.

Amane averted his eyes, concluding that it was a mistake to even expect such words from her. But Mahiru did not look away.

"You are attractive."

Amane couldn't believe his ears when he heard these clearly enunciated words.

"To be honest, you are cute, but you're also cool. More than anyone else, in my eyes."

"...You don't have to force yourself to flatter me."

"How rude. What would I get out of lying to you? I'm just saying what I think."

"...You're overstating it, and you have no taste in men."

Amane was working on becoming a better version of himself, but he didn't think he was especially desirable. So even when Mahiru praised him, he couldn't let himself believe her. Especially after she went on and on about how he was cute.

"So what is your definition of 'cool,' Amane?"

Amane was frowning, and Mahiru gently gazed at him.

"For me, I think to view a guy as charming, you need to take everything about his personality into account, from the aura around him, to how he carries himself, to his words, actions, and expressions. Thinking that attractiveness is only a matter of appearance seems very superficial to me."

"W-well, that's true, but—"

"Looking at you objectively, I wouldn't say you're handsome enough to captivate everyone who looks at you. But your face is well-proportioned, and like I said before, appearances aren't the only thing that make someone appealing. You're maybe a little sarcastic, but you're always polite, and you're well-mannered and gentlemanly and kind. You're always reaching out to those in need even though you put on a show of being cold and distant. You're cautious, but you're dependable when you need to be. Looking at you all together, you are attractive, Amane. Of course, I can't deny that my subjective opinion and personal preferences factor into that assessment, but you're very cool, so please have a little more confidence."

"Th-that's enough, I get it, I hear you, so—"

"You don't get it. You don't have any self-confidence, so if I don't get serious and tell you—"

"I said that's enough!"

Mahiru had gotten more insistent as she spoke, and before she even finished, Amane had found himself groaning with embarrassment. If Mahiru flattered him any further, he felt like he would burst into tears of shame, so he had to do something to stop her from continuing to list his various merits. He took a deep breath to try to somehow calm his heart, which was sending heat radiating up to his face, as if he wasn't embarrassed enough already. He felt like his cheeks probably looked as red as ripe apples, and that even Mahiru, who had just been praising him, would find it pathetic.

The fact that Mahiru held Amane in high regard had somehow sunk in—it was clear to him, so he didn't need her to continue in any more detail. Her compliments only made him heartsick. He felt such joy and shame at the idea that she valued him at all that he couldn't stand to be there any longer. He wanted to run away.

Amane's eyes darted around as he desperately tried to shake off the heat and humiliation that had overtaken his body.

Mahiru looked at him and smiled broadly, obviously delighted. "...That is what's so cute about you, Amane."

It was a little late, but Amane finally understood what Mahiru was trying to say. He glared at her; his face still flushed red.

"If you try to say anything more, I'll have to stop you somehow."

"...Oh, and how will you do that?"

"What do you mean, how? I'll manage, I'm sure."

"Well, you don't scare me one bit."

Mahiru didn't look like she was going to restrain herself. Still smiling, she gently reached out toward Amane's face.

He could feel Mahiru's chilly fingers pressingagainst his feverish cheeks. Gently, she turned his face so that he was looking directly at her.

"...No matter what you say, even if you don't think it's true, to me, you are attractive, Amane. You don't have to worry about it; I can see all the best parts of you."

She was very close to him, and her voice was bright like the rays of the spring sun, refreshing and clear. Her words slowly caressed his heart as she softly praised him. The warmth and affection in her caramel-colored eyes took his breath away, as they reflected him and him alone.

...I can't...

Amane felt a heat that he'd never experienced before. He couldn't so much as manage a groan, or even to avert his eyes. He just stood there, basking in Mahiru's radiance.

Then, suddenly, Mahiru's smile changed to something much softer.

"You're adorable."

The moment he heard her sweetly whisper, a pleasant tingle ran up his spine, and the warmth heating Amane's whole body grew even stronger under Mahiru's gaze.

Before he realized it, he had grasped her delicate fingers and taken them off his cheek, and in a single, smooth movement, had pressed Mahiru against the back of the couch, bringing his face very close to hers.

There was only a palm's breadth of distance between them.

Amane had kept his word, closing Mahiru's mouth shut with his hand against her lips as he stared down at her.

The caramel-colored eyes peeking through long eyelashes that almost looked like a hazy curtain were open wide in surprise.

That was close, Amane thought.

If she had looked at him with those eyes, if she had stirred him up any further, he might have lost all restraint for a moment. If he didn't exert the small amount of self-control he had in order to stop her, they both would have given up their first kiss.

As much as he would have liked to keep going and gradually chip away at those "firsts," Amane was brought back to reality by the urgent alarm bells of reason ringing in his head. He was grateful that he had chosen a course of action that he wouldn't regret later.

Mahiru, who had been calm and collected until a moment prior, stiffened when he touched her lips, and a light crimson color spread over her cheeks in an instant.

Amane smirked when he saw that she hadn't gotten any better at dealing with sudden surprises. Slowly, he lifted his hand from her lips.

They were still close enough that if he'd wiggled his fingers a little, they'd have brushed her face, but instead of pulling back a little, he slowly put his lips near her ear and whispered, "…If you say something like that again, I'll pull my hand away, and really shut your mouth."

Though he couldn't see her face, Amane could feel Mahiru shudder.

However, she didn't push him away or try to block him. Feeling relieved, Amane gradually backed away. He was suddenly embarrassed at how much he wanted to see Mahiru's face, and he guiltily looked away.

In fact, he was already feeling intensely ashamed over his sudden, reckless boldness, and he moved to rise from the sofa. He knew that he wasn't thinking straight, and that what he needed was to get some actual, physical distance from her for a moment.

But when he started to stand, he felt some resistance. He looked down to where he felt something pulling on him, then the next moment, a sweet smell filled his nose.

In the blink of an eye, threads of shimmering gold danced past him, and he felt something soft graze one of his still-flushed cheeks.

Then he heard the sound of slippers on the floor and the echo of footsteps that were wilder and more restless than they were nimble. Mahiru was gone, and it was like everything he had just felt had been an illusion.

He recognized the bang of his front door slamming shut, and Amane brought his hand to the cheek where something soft had touched it.

"—Why?" he mumbled, but naturally there was no answer.

Sapped of all energy, spirit, and composure, Amane sunk down into the sofa and stared down the hallway where the flaxen whirlwind had disappeared.

Mahiru did not return to Amane's apartment for the rest of the day.

Chapter 12

Pretending Not to See, Pretending Not to Know

What was it that had touched his cheek?

After it happened, Mahiru did not return to Amane's apartment. He did not see her for the rest of the day. Except for when he was sleeping—to be accurate, he had been too distressed for to sleep, but he'd dozed off a few times—any time he wasn't, he was turning over Mahiru's actions in his mind.

It had only been for a moment, brief enough to make him question whether it had been his imagination—but something soft had definitely grazed his cheek. Knowing how close she'd been to him at the time, and remembering the feel of it, Amane could guess what Mahiru had done. But that didn't mean he understood it.

No one would ever have imagined it, that Mahiru herself would kiss him, even if it was just his cheek.

…Why?

Typically, a kiss is something only shared with someone close or important. Amane wanted to tell Mahiru how precious she was to him, but his last attempt had gone so poorly that he was embarrassed just thinking about it.

There was really no excuse—he hadn't even tried to make a move.

However, Mahiru was different. Even if it was only his cheek, she had really kissed him.

He understood that she cared about him, liked him even, and treated him well. But confronted with her feelings in the form of a kiss, Amane was left more bewildered than elated.

I wonder if she's starting to really like me?

Amane felt like he'd never gotten the chance to really impress her, like she'd only ever seen what a worthless person he was. He couldn't think of any reason why she would like him.

The notion that nobody could ever fall for him, and that he was an arrogant fool for hoping, spun round and round in Amane's head, making it hard to think about anything else.

At school, he kept his mess of emotions from showing on his face, but inside, he was miserably distressed.

Whenever Mahiru made eye contact with Amane during school, she would turn her gaze away subtly, so he also avoided looking in her direction.

Nevertheless, Amane's eyes followed Mahiru whenever possible, and the ever-perceptive Itsuki must have noticed the small distance that had opened between Amane and Mahiru.

"Did the two of you get into a fight?" Itsuki asked over lunch.

"Huh? You had a fight, Fujimiya?" Yuuta asked.

Chitose and Mahiru weren't joining them that day, so the three boys were having lunch together.

"No, we're not fighting, but...well, um, something, some things happened..."

He mumbled those words and avoided going into detail. Amane couldn't possibly explain that he had completely failed to kiss Mahiru, and that she had kissed him on the cheek instead.

Itsuki did not hide his exasperation. He gave Amane a look that said, *"You better give up and confess everything if you know what's good for you."*

Amane couldn't meet his friend's gaze. "Anyway...," he muttered, "some things happened, and we're both feeling self-conscious about it, or like..."

"Unbelievable, just how much of a wuss are you?"

"Shut up, man."

"Now, now, Fujimiya strikes me as the cautious type," Yuuta interjected. "I doubt he can make an approach without a painfully obvious signal telling him to go for it."

"That's what I mean; he always chickens out!"

There was no way Itsuki and Yuuta could understand what had happened, but the two of them didn't hold back, and their accusations at Amane for "chickening out" stung quite a bit.

"...It's just, the idea of someone liking me—like, if I was more self-confident, this wouldn't be so hard, and... If I was better-looking, I would feel more confident, but..."

"Fujimiya, if anything, you're a high-quality guy who acts like a loser despite everything you've got going for you."

"I don't know what to do with that, coming from you, Kadowaki, the crème de la crème."

If Amane had been as accomplished as Yuuta, and had good looks to boot, he wouldn't have struggled so much. He might have been able to accept Mahiru's affection without a second thought and confess his feelings for her. He would have been able to stand proudly by her side, without having to work for it.

He understood that Mahiru had been sincere when she'd said that he was attractive, but objective and subjective opinions were two very different things.

Mahiru's subjective opinion was the most important, of course, but when he thought about all their peers watching, as well as his own self-worth, he felt like he had a lot of improvement left to make.

"I'm not saying that I'm jealous of your looks, Kadowaki, but if I had those going for me, I'm sure I would be more confident."

Amane's hesitation and anxiety were his own fault. It was the fear of reaching out to her that kept him stuck, worrying over answers that he might never even get, all because he lacked any kind of mental fortitude.

"It's a little late, but you need to have some faith in yourself and make a move!"

"I told you, I'm working on it now. I'm gonna make a move soon, but…"

Amane was working on building up his confidence. He was working hard in school by being diligent with his studies so that he could maintain his position in the top ten.

Amane had a good memory and learned new things easily, so he counted himself lucky that he could keep up his grades without working too hard. After that, he just had to keep raising the bar.

The problem was going to be exercise.

Amane wished he had some sort of athletic prowess, like Yuuta for example. But he was just average. If anything, he was a bit of a bookworm, so he wasn't expecting to accomplish anything amazing.

He'd been exercising in order to look better, even just a little, and to improve his health and self-confidence. However, he had been focusing on physical fitness and not doing the sort of training that one needed to excel at any particular sport.

Amane was feeling down about himself, musing that if only he were a bit more athletic, he might be able to play a more active role in the following month's Sports Day events.

"Leaving aside what just happened, I'm going to do my best and proceed at my own pace, so please don't rush me too much."

"Okay, if that's what you really want," Yuuta agreed. "But...we're getting impatient watching you, you know."

Itsuki grinned. "Speaking of which, when do we convene the next meeting of the 'kick Amane's butt into gear' club?"

Amane's cheek twitched at the idea that the two of them were planning something. "Seriously, what have you guys got up your sleeves?"

Yuuta only shrugged and smiled and said uneasily, "Look, we just mean that we're rooting for you, so..."

Amane spent the whole day at school worrying about the true meaning behind Mahiru's kiss. Then, after heading home, he waited for her in his apartment, growing ever more anxious.

Mahiru had responded as soon as he messaged her asking if she was coming over, so he knew she was on her way, but Amane felt quite nervous about it.

It would be their first time talking since the events of the day before, and the strain was making Amane's heart and stomach ache.

He was practically writhing in pain on the sofa, too focused on the sound of the ticking clock as he waited for her, when he finally heard the lock in his front door turn.

Amane felt himself jump at the noise, but he knew that if he showed any agitation, Mahiru would get agitated, too. They wouldn't be able to talk, so he did what he could to suppress his nervousness. Taking deep breaths, Amane waited for her to approach, and eventually, she appeared before him.

Though he felt somewhat hesitant, he looked up and saw Mahiru, who had changed into her regular clothes, standing there as always... no, standing there with slightly pink cheeks, as her eyes darted around nervously.

"...Um, I'm sorry about yesterday," she said. "About leaving before dinner."

"Oh, no, I'm not worried about that, so...," he answered awkwardly.

With stiff movements, like a machine that needed oil, Mahiru took a seat beside him on the sofa.

Even though she sat next to him like usual, he noticed that she was sitting on the very edge of the couch, as if trying to keep her distance from Amane, and hugging a cushion.

She looked as uncomfortable as he felt.

It was a little lonely to have her so far away after he'd gotten used to her sitting right beside him, but on the other hand, he felt relieved to have some distance between them.

"So about that thing...the thing that happened yesterday..."

After a brief silence, Mahiru broached the topic hesitantly, shaking so much that her long flaxen hair formed undulating waves of gold.

"...Uhh, M-Mahiru...why, why did you do that?"

Amane knew he was being vague, but he was too nervous to ask the question he really wanted to ask, so he tried to probe indirectly.

In response to Amane's timid inquiry, Mahiru pursed her lips and looked at him. Her eyes were cloudy, and she looked dissatisfied, and then began to speak slowly.

"I—I just got caught up in the moment. Or maybe...it was revenge."

"Revenge?"

"I mean, you're the one who started it, aren't you?"

"A-ah, well, maybe that's true, but..."

The big difference was that he hadn't gone all the way, whereas Mahiru had actually kissed him. But Amane was worried she might retreat if he pointed that out, so he swallowed his words.

"Well then, I had the right to do it, too, didn't I?"

"...That's not the issue. Um..."

Are you glad that you kissed me, even if it was on the cheek?

If he could only have asked her directly, his worries would have ended right there.

He knew for certain that Mahiru hadn't avoided the...thing he'd almost done. That she didn't hate the thought of kissing him, either.

The only piece of information missing was how she really felt about it.

It was not impossible for Amane to guess what the answer might be. Only, he was afraid of outright rejection and couldn't bring himself to ask.

I'm so pathetic.

As Amane groaned to himself about how sad and hopeless he felt, he noticed that Mahiru was blushing faintly. She saw him looking and stared right back at him.

"What is it?" she asked.

"...Nothing," was his only response.

Then Amane turned away so that he couldn't see her anymore.

Chapter 13

Sports Day Preparations and New Friends

"Aww, I'm on the red team!" Chitose whined mournfully when she saw the announcement about the upcoming Sports Day.

Itsuki had already seen the results and knew that he had been assigned the white team, making them opponents for once. "If they're going to the trouble of dividing us up, they could have at least put us on the teams that match our names…" He groaned.

"Either way, you'd still be on different teams," Yuuta reminded him.

Itsuki's surname was Akazawa, which contained the character for *red*, and Chitose's was Shirakawa, which contained the character for *white*. At school, they were sometimes called the "red and white couple."

"That's true…it's really tragic…a forbidden love, two people drawn to each other despite being on opposing sides…"

Not bothering to hide his exasperation at the two who were lamenting their fates as yet another way to flirt with each other, Amane gazed at the paper that showed how the students were divided up.

Amane was on the red team with Yuuta and Chitose, while Itsuki and Mahiru had been assigned to the white team. Although that meant Amane would be with the track and field ace, it appeared that the opposing side included more members from the school sports clubs overall.

Amane didn't particularly care whether his team won or lost, but he did want to put on a good show for Mahiru.

"What events do you want, Amane?" Itsuki asked when he'd finished flirting with Chitose.

He and Chitose were on the class's Sports Day executive committee together. It was exactly the sort of thing that a popular, energetic guy like Itsuki would sign up for. He was famous for avoiding putting too much effort into anything, which confused Amane as to why his friend took on so many class leadership roles.

"What events are there, again?"

"The events left are the sprints, relays, obstacle course, scavenger hunt, three-legged race, ball toss, and tug-of-war. I'm guessing the interclass relay isn't of much interest to a member of the 'go-home club' like you."

"I guess the ball toss would be good."

"Of course you'd go for the most boring one... Well, just remember you have to do at least two activities."

"All right, I want the ball toss and the scavenger hunt."

He didn't want to embarrass himself in front of Mahiru, and Amane had a feeling that the relays and the sprints would be dominated by the members of the athletic clubs.

Itsuki, who he would normally pair up with for the three-legged race, was on the opposing team, and although Amane had Yuuta, he didn't have the confidence that he could keep up with him, given his strength and speed.

So he chose the easier events, and Itsuki put on a bitter smile.

"You're really going for the boring ones, huh...? But you know, depending on what happens, the scavenger hunt race might be really exciting."

"Well, I don't do a lot of running, so…"

"You never change!"

Amane wanted to avoid any direct competition against the sports clubs and figured participating in the games meant for the students in the cultural clubs was the safest option.

"The problem is the cavalry battle with all the guys…," he said. "You're on the opposing team, after all."

The only guys in his class who Amane was especially good friends with were Itsuki and Yuuta. He figured that Yuuta might let him join his team out of pity, but even if he did, Amane suspected that he would end up feeling a little isolated.

Since most boys would form teams with their friends, Amane, who prided himself on being a wallflower, usually wasn't enthusiastic about Sports Day.

"Ah, if that's the problem, you should be fine."

"Hmm?"

"Yuuta, Kazu, and Makoto said they wanted you to join them. There, speak of the devils…"

When Amane looked to where Itsuki was pointing, he saw three boys waving their hands at him. It was Kadowaki and two other boys he seldom talked to.

Still, Amane knew of them. They were good friends of Yuuta's, and he'd pointed them out once with a smile, telling Amane, "Now that we hang out, I want you to get to know my buddies."

One of them, the one Itsuki had called Kazu, was a serious-looking guy who was in the track and field club with Yuuta, and he specialized in long-distance running. His full name was Kazuya Hiiragi.

The other boy was Makoto Kokonoe. He had a comparatively small build and, according to the girls, something of a fickle nature.

When Yuuta wasn't hanging out with Amane and the others, he was with them.

"Hey, Fujimiya! Come over here. Let's form a cavalry battle team!" In the middle of the group, Yuuta was calling him over with his usual refreshing smile.

Amane hesitated, but Itsuki said, "Get going," and physically pushed him from the back. He stumbled up to the group, and Yuuta welcomed him with another grin.

"You're not teamed up with anyone yet, right, Fujimiya?" Yuuta asked. "If you want, we'd like you to be in our group."

"That's fine by me, but what about the other two guys?"

"I don't mind." The first one to answer was Makoto. "Yuuta and Kazuya are both tall, so height-wise, we think you'd be the best addition."

"Ah, I see..."

Makoto was probably the one who was going to ride on top of everybody's shoulders, so it made sense that he was looking for three people with similar statures.

Amane was on the tall side, not that different from Yuuta and Kazuya when they lined up next to each other. Although he was much ganglier and didn't have much in the way of sturdiness and resilience like the other two did.

"You okay with this, Hiiragi?" Yuuta asked.

"Yeah, isn't that why we called him over here? And also because I'm curious about him, since you said you guys are friends now."

"Don't worry," Yuuta assured him. "Fujimiya's a good guy."

Kazuya stared at Amane. "Sure, your judgment is always spot-on, Yuuta. I've got no reservations. That said, since it was your idea to team up with him, I won't know how I feel for sure until we spend some time together."

Amane smiled bleakly at the questionable statement. Kazuya was still looking him over, and it made him somewhat uncomfortable.

That said, since he'd just entered a new social group, he expected a certain amount of scrutiny.

"Well, welcome aboard," Hiiragi said finally.

It seemed like Amane had passed muster, at least enough that they weren't going to turn him away. The other boys gave him mellow smiles, and Amane also smiled and responded, "Happy to join the group."

"So I've got a question," Makoto said. "Are you close friends with Shiina, Fujimiya?"

At Yuuta's suggestion, the team was having a small get-together at a fast-food restaurant. As he munched on his chicken nuggets, Makoto sounded like the question had just occurred to him.

Amane quickly stuffed his face with french fries, hoping to avoid making any embarrassing expressions.

The four of them were at a fast-food restaurant because Yuuta had wanted to discuss strategies for the cavalry battle...but his main motive was to try and develop their friendship.

Amane had never expected someone who was still a relative stranger to ask something like that.

He shot a glance over at Yuuta and received an innocent look, so Amane figured that the question must have come purely from Makoto's observations.

That meant Amane would need to work hard not to let anything show on his face, if he could.

"What makes you think that?" he asked dryly.

"Well, the five of you, Yuuta included, are always chatting and doing stuff together. But Shiina behaves sort of differently with you than with Itsuki and Yuuta."

"Oh, does she? I hadn't noticed at all."

Kazuya looked over at Amane like he hadn't expected that answer—his eyes were open wide in pure surprise. "I don't think anyone has really picked up on it, either. Everyone else has just been watching your little group out of simple jealousy."

"That's disturbing to hear..."

"Well, from the way you're acting, I bet I'm right."

Amane wasn't sure how to answer Makoto's questions. The other boy's expression was practically unreadable. Amane looked over at Yuuta for help, and Yuuta gave him a look that said that these guys could be trusted.

Amane scratched his cheek as he thought it over. Makoto seemed convinced that he was right, but Amane didn't want those ideas to spread much.

However, Yuuta seemed like a good judge of character, and Makoto's question seemed to stem from pure curiosity rather than invasive prying—he didn't seem to mean anything by it.

"...Well, I guess you could say that we're good friends."

"It seems like she enjoys your attention, so I guess that must be true."

"...Is that what it looks like?"

"More or less."

Makoto's powers of observation were truly frightening.

Amane decided that, rather than clumsily dodging the question, it would invite less suspicion to tell a certain amount of the truth. It was probably more believable to admit to the friendship.

"We simply happen to live in the same neighborhood, so we had the chance to talk and became friendly, that's all."

"And you've been friends since before our second year, right?"

"Well...second year was when we started hanging out together at school."

Naturally, Amane couldn't tell him that Mahiru was his next-door neighbor, and that she came over to his apartment every day and fixed his meals. Even though his answer wasn't exactly accurate, he decided there only needed to be a hint of truth to it.

After Amane answered, Makoto looked at Yuuta. "Did you know about this?"

Yuuta nodded, probably figuring that there was no need to hide it now that Amane had said something.

Makoto sighed softly. "What the heck... What fools we were."

"Fools?" Amane asked.

"Oh, I'm talking about myself... Yuuta, you hid this from us, didn't you?"

"Indeed," Yuuta answered, "because I couldn't tell you anything until Fujimiya said something first. But I didn't think for a second that you and Kazuya would spread rumors."

"Of course not," Kazuya confirmed. "I'm not gonna go out of my way to do something that will make people hate me."

"That honesty of yours is a virtue, Kazuya." Yuuta beamed.

Kazuya tilted his head in confusion—he didn't seem to understand why Yuuta was complimenting him for something so basic. Amane knew then that he didn't have to doubt Kazuya's good intentions.

He did feel like he was taking a bit of a risk by sharing all this information, but he felt confident that he was opening up to decent people.

Amane was really impressed with Kazuya, who had a reputation of being an upstanding guy. He was serious in a totally different manner from Yuuta. Amane understood keenly why Kazuya was one of Yuuta's best friends.

Kazuya also had a very good eye for people's character. As a friend and as a companion, Amane doubted he had any serious shortcomings.

"So in other words, it would be best if I didn't tell anyone about this, right?"

"Well, I don't expect you to lie, but I think it would probably be best if you could pretend you don't know anyway. That said, if someone were to ask about our friendship, I think they're more likely to ask Itsuki or Yuuta, rather than come to you, Kazuya."

"You're not wrong there," Yuuta chuckled quietly. Amane felt reassured by his friend's remark.

"Anyway, if you could do that for me, I'd be very grateful," he said. "I don't want to cause problems for her, after all."

Amane would have preferred to cover up the whole affair, and he hoped the others would keep it to themselves.

"I'm sure she wouldn't like it if all her friends started asking her all sorts of questions, either. So I want to keep it on the down low. For her sake as well as mine."

Amane knew that if their secret was revealed, he would be the target of a great deal of jealousy, and he was prepared for that. However, Mahiru would have to answer all kinds of insensitive questions. The biggest question: Why him?

To their classmates, Mahiru was not just a gifted student...she was almost a divine being, an object of worship in their school. There would be much confusion and plenty of criticism about a member of the campus nobility associating with an ordinary plebeian.

Their curiosity might be completely rational, but they would probably make Mahiru uncomfortable all the same. He recalled her saying once that she wanted to be able to choose her relationships freely. And Amane was convinced that Mahiru would get angry with him for embarrassing her.

Since he didn't want to do anything that might upset her, he'd tried to hide their friendship for as long as possible.

...Though I get the feeling that she wants to go public...

Amane had suspected that recently she'd been trying to close the distance between them, little by little, but had chalked it up to his imagination.

"Ohh, ahh..."

"What is it, Kokonoe?"

"...Never mind, I just sort of realized something. It must be hard, man."

Makoto was looking at Amane with a bewildered expression. Amane could only tilt his head in confusion.

"Yuuta, is this by any chance...?" Makoto asked vaguely.

"That's right." Yuuta nodded.

"What is?" Kazuya wondered aloud. "What are you talking about?"

"I don't think it would make any sense to you, Kazuya; don't worry about it," Makoto insisted.

Kazuya didn't seem upset at his friend for brushing him off. Instead, he smiled. "In that case, I guess I don't need to know." His reaction showed the depths of their trust and the strength of their friendship.

For some reason, Yuuta and Makoto nodded knowingly. Amane wondered what the two of them were thinking and wore a puzzled expression as he continued picking at his french fries.

"Mahiru, what events did you choose for Sports Day?"

As she was putting leftovers from dinner, packed in Tupperware, into the fridge and was about to take ice cream out of the freezer, Amane asked Mahiru this question.

Some time had passed since the incident with the kiss, and while things between Amane and Mahiru had more or less settled down, the subtle awkwardness between them had yet to completely dissipate.

No matter what they did, the two were both still extremely

conscious of what had happened. There was a distance between them that hadn't been there before. They were back to sitting next to each other, but with enough space that they wouldn't accidentally touch.

The atmosphere over dinner that night was also a little tense, though still amicable. Even though things between them weren't exactly strained, it was clear that they were both overly conscious of each other.

After passing the spoon for ice cream to Amane, she looked up in an attempt to remember.

"Let me see...I chose the relay and the scavenger hunt."

"Oh, same here. But instead of the relay, I asked for the ball toss."

Amane didn't know whether he would get his top choices, but the ball toss was honestly not very popular, so he figured it was likely he would.

It was a little iffy whether he would get the scavenger hunt, but even if he ended up with his third choice, the obstacle course, that was okay with him.

That event tested a competitor's sense of balance and flexibility more than pure leg strength, so even though Amane was not particularly fast, he probably wouldn't drag his team down.

"You really don't like sports, do you?"

"Leave it to the pros. I'm just not that athletic, is all."

"...If I'm not mistaken, your grades in gym are about average, right?"

"Unfortunately, yeah."

Amane imagined he'd probably have better scores in gym class if he were more athletically inclined, but sadly, sports were not his forte. He wasn't so awful that he'd call it a weakness—he was comfortable being simply average.

The notion that he might excel in sports as well as academics seemed like a dream for Amane, unlike Yuuta and Mahiru, both of whom had natural talent and worked hard.

"...If you were to be honest, you hate Sports Day, don't you, Amane?"

"Well, it's not that I necessarily hate exercise, but I do hate it when it's mandatory. I like exercising on my own time, by myself."

As they made their way back to the living room sofa, Amane recalled a bitter memory of a winter marathon he had run once. It wasn't that he lacked the endurance—he could run the distances they did in gym class. He simply didn't find timed races to be all that interesting.

It felt nicer just to run, at his own pace, toward his own goals, so it made sense that he wasn't a fan of structured races.

Mahiru smiled sadly as she watched Amane take the lid off the ice cream with a bitter look on his face.

"It's not like I don't understand," she said sympathetically. "I also don't really enjoy doing something if I've been forced to do it."

"Right? So that's why I'm just going to do enough to contribute."

Amane didn't want to slack off enough to invite any negative attention, and he knew he'd feel guilty if he didn't do his part. He wasn't going to go all out, but he would at least do enough to demonstrate that he was capable. Though if he ended up getting the events he'd requested, he figured he wouldn't have to try particularly hard anyway.

"Heh-heh, too bad I won't get to see you going all out."

"Leave it to me, I'll show you what I can do during the ball toss... probably."

"Probably?"

"Well, it's a boring event, so I won't stand out much."

Now that they were in high school, Amane didn't even under-stand why a childish event like the ball toss was kept as part of the program. Surely there were some schools where it had been phased out, but their school kept it nonetheless.

It was probably there to give the nonathletes a chance, but even so, Amane had gotten the impression that nobody got too worked up over the ball toss.

"You have a fairly good aim when you're throwing things, Amane. Your shooting was on-target when you played basketball in the gym the other day, and I've never seen you miss when you throw a tissue or something into the trash. That's just because you're too lazy to get up, though." Mahiru added a quiet jab at the end.

All Amane could do was force a smile.

"Please forgive me for being so lazy, since I never miss the trash can."

"Well, I suppose it's fine since you're in your own home. But I'm serious, you know, your aim is quite good."

"I guess I'm all right at throwing things. Especially stuff like darts. My mom took me along with her all the time."

Amane's mother had dragged her son around with her to all sorts of places, and he'd picked up a number of useless skills—everything from Airsoft tournaments, to white water rafting, to darts matches, bowling contests, and game centers.

Apparently, they were finally going to come in handy, so he supposed he shouldn't call them completely useless.

"Don't you feel like you got a special education of sorts, Amane?"

"Maybe, but only in the field of games."

"That's amazing in a way, and so is Shihoko."

Mahiru sounded more impressed than amazed, but Amane, as the person who'd been dragged around, wasn't sure he agreed with her sentiment.

But it was true that he owed a lot to his mother.

She had packed his days with all sorts of novel experiences, and during his middle school years, when he'd gone through a difficult period, that had never changed. She'd always made time for him. That had really helped him through his depression. Nevertheless, it had been exhausting, being pulled from one place to the next, and he hadn't always appreciated it.

"…Well, the event is what it is, and I doubt it will be especially exciting to watch. I'll put in as much effort as I need to. It's gonna be pretty boring, though," he concluded, then stuck his spoon into his partially melted ice cream and scooped up a bite.

The rich cacao ice cream was lightly sweetened, a limited-edition flavor made for convenience stores by a famous chocolate company. It was one of the more expensive ice creams on the market, so Amane wanted to savor every last morsel.

"Do you really hate Sports Day that much?"

"No, I just kind of hate spending half a day outside in my gym clothes now that it's gotten hot. Though I guess we'll have tents."

"Well, when you put it that way, I can see your point. But you'd better do your best, okay?"

"I'll do what I have to."

"Geez."

Mahiru pouted but then her gaze was drawn to the spoon or, to be more accurate, to the ice cream. Amane couldn't help but laugh.

Thinking that he should have bought a second one just for Mahiru, since she liked sweets so much, he held the spoon up in front of her for her to try a bite. Her eyes sparkled enthusiastically.

She's really much easier to read than she used to be, huh?

Chuckling quietly, Amane brought the spoon closer to Mahiru's lips, and she took the spoon into her mouth without hesitation, like a kitten accepting food from the hand of its owner.

Her eyes closed in a satisfied smile.

The ice cream was delicious. He could tell by her expression.

Amane thought so, too, but Mahiru's tongue was more sensitive than most people's. She was an excellent judge when it came to a food's quality and flavor. If she said that something looked tasty, she was probably right.

"...This is the good stuff, isn't it?"

"You can tell?"

"I mean, it's obvious from the packaging. But it's even tastier than I expected."

"Is it? Here."

When he offered her another bite, she accepted it gladly.

Faced with a smile warm enough to melt ice cream right out of the freezer, Amane felt his face slowly heating up.

...Crap, I just fed her like it was the most natural thing in the world.

He'd been trying his best to keep a bit of distance between them, yet he'd gone and done that without thinking about it.

He thought they were both to blame, though, since Mahiru had shown him such an unguarded expression, despite how things had been between them lately. But he wouldn't have expected her to be happy about being spoon-fed by some guy.

"...Mahiru, you can have the rest."

"Huh?"

"I'm brewing some coffee, so I'm good. It's all yours."

Amane pushed the ice cream cup and spoon at Mahiru, who looked confused, and then escaped to the kitchen, where he desperately shoved a filter and some coffee beans into the coffee maker.

©Hanekoto

Chapter 14

Saying Goodbye to My Cowardly Self

Early June—Amane's school held their Sports Day during the time of year when the weather starts becoming more humid.

Unlike Field Day in elementary and middle school, high school Sports Day wasn't much of a harmonious and happy event—if anything, it was more like an extension of their usual gym class. No parents or guardians came to cheer them on.

Even so, it was one of the few yearly events run by the school, and a certain part of the student body was always filled with excitement. Especially the underclassmen in the athletic clubs, as they always eagerly embraced the opportunity to show off their abilities to their upperclassmen.

On the other hand, most of the students who belonged to cultural clubs showed no interest at all.

Amane, a member of the so-called "go-home club," fit best in the second group.

"What a pain."

Amane smiled secretly to himself when he heard another student in the same tent with him grumble quietly.

Although similarly uninterested in the happenings, Amane

wasn't so put off that he was going to let it show. Instead, he'd chosen to maintain a composed expression.

Fortunately, he had been assigned to the events he'd requested and wasn't going to end up running around in circles or anything. The only running around he was going to be doing would be during the cavalry battle that all the boys were going to take part in.

Yuuta, who was on the same red team as Amane and who was sitting in the tent with him, gave Amane a look of surprise. "You don't seem that unhappy, Fujimiya. I thought for sure you hated this stuff."

"Well, I got the events I wanted, and I don't have anything else to do now, so it's not so bad. Though I do think that studying would be more fun."

"I think that's a pretty unusual opinion, I'd imagine..."

Kazuya had overheard them from nearby. "Seems like Fujimiya's excellent grades are balanced out by not being so great at sports," he said. "Guess that's how it goes sometimes."

Amane couldn't deny that and smiled bitterly. It was the truth, but having someone else point it out gave him mixed feelings. He appreciated the compliment regarding his academic abilities, but he couldn't help but long to excel in both school and sports.

"I've been good about following the training regimen that Kadowaki gave me, but I've been thinking maybe I should put together a slightly more demanding program," Amane said.

"Hmm, well, the workout that we do is meant for athletes, so I think you should stick with your current program, if you're just training for your health," Yuuta replied. "If we lived a little closer together, I would go jogging and stuff with you, though."

"There's no way that I could match your speed and strength, Kadowaki."

"He's right," Makoto said with a weary look on his face. "Don't you remember how I almost died when I went with you, Yuuta? You don't go jogging, you go running." He had accompanied Yuuta on runs before.

Makoto wasn't one of the sports club types; he was actually a member of the astronomy club. He was slim, small enough to be described as dainty, and his skin was pale. He didn't look like he was capable of much exertion.

That said, Amane knew that dainty and small Mahiru was capable of intense exercise, so the rule didn't always hold.

"Nah, I think Fujimiya can do it," Yuuta said. "Sounds like you didn't get that tired when you used to run marathons and stuff."

"I've been training recently, working hard so that I don't get weak when I get older, but I'm no match for a real athlete!"

"You are the only one who's already thinking about getting old..."

"You're a strange guy, Fujimiya. No, maybe I should say you're an interesting guy."

"Was that supposed to be a compliment?"

Kazuya has an honest, sincere personality, and his way of speaking is straightforward. He's direct and doesn't hold back.

Amane had come to understand this since they started hanging out.

"I'm pretty sure that was supposed to be a compliment," Yuuta answered for him.

"In that case, thanks."

"Don't mention it."

"What are you all even talking about...?"

Makoto wasn't trying to hide his exasperation, but there wasn't any ridicule in his words either, just simple frustration, as well as a slight tinge of genuine amusement.

"Now, now. Kazuya has always been a bit of an airhead," Yuuta said.

"I don't think I'm an airhead..."

"That's 'cause the person in question is the only one who can't tell. It's fine, Kazuya, don't worry about it. You're perfect just the way you are."

"Hmph. Really?"

Kazuya seemed happy to accept that answer and didn't argue any further.

"You're okay with that...?" Amane mumbled, and looked toward the sports grounds.

Out on the field, students had been running the short distance races.

Judging from the length of the track, they were doing the hundred-meter dash. The first heat seemed to have finished already, and the second one was starting to line up.

The next heat was a girls' group, and there were a few fast girls on the red team, including a familiar face with reddish-brown hair.

"I thought Chitose quit the track and field club. Is she really that fast?" Amane asked.

"Yeah, Shirakawa is really fast," Yuuta answered. "In middle school, she was a track club ace, you know."

"Huh, really?"

"Mm. Though she didn't join the club in high school. She said it was a pain in the butt always fighting with the upperclassmen."

"I guess this is where I make a joke about what caused the fights?"

"Well, hmm, there's kind of a story behind it...but I guess you could say she got discouraged or just tired of it."

"...Tired?"

"There were issues when she started dating Itsuki. How should I explain it...? Well, there was an upperclassman on the track team who also liked Itsuki, see, and on top of that, Shirakawa's times were faster than theirs... It created some tension, and one thing led to another, get it?"

"Ah, I see now."

The two of them were well known in their grade as a couple, but Amane had heard from Itsuki that during middle school, before they'd started dating, he had pursued Chitose fervently.

Apparently, Chitose had had a much cooler personality back then, and it had taken Itsuki quite some time to convince her to go out with him.

It wasn't difficult to imagine the upperclassman fighting with Chitose over Itsuki once she realized what was going on.

"She said that all the obligations of a club were annoying and decided not to join, I guess. But you know, she still likes running because I often spot her running on the weekends."

Yuuta added that they lived in the same neighborhood, then smiled and looked over at Chitose, who had taken her stance for a crouching start.

From Amane's perspective as a near beginner, Chitose's stance seemed masterful, even beautiful.

Her expression, seen from a distance, was not her usual carefree joking smile but a sharp and serious look.

The sound of the start gun echoed across the grounds.

The moment it did, Chitose was off, sprinting faster than anyone else.

She ran like the wind, with a form that anyone would have agreed was lovely to watch, leaving even the current members of the track and field club behind.

Her hair streamed behind her in soft waves as her body moved intently forward. Her feet pounded the ground with surprising force as she headed for the goal, faster than any of the other runners.

Amane watched transfixed as Chitose cut through the goal tape before he even knew it.

Chitose, who had run the course the fastest, held up the first-place flag and looked toward the red team…toward where Amane was, with a big grin.

Waving the flag in the air with satisfaction, she made even him feel happy to be part of the team.

Once the hundred-meter dash was over and Chitose came back to the tent, she had her chest puffed up with pride.

"I'm baaack! Did you see me?"

"We did, we did. You were fast!"

"Yay, thanks!"

"You sure were. It feels great to watch you run, Shirakawa."

Chitose looked very pleased to receive compliments from two current members of the track and field club.

Even Amane offered some words of praise. "Good job, you were flying."

She had been so much faster than he had expected that he could scarcely believe it. But Chitose didn't seem all that excited about it. She smiled in a carefree manner. "Ahh, that was fun."

She looked more like herself, without any air of tension about her. It was completely different than how she'd looked while she was running. Amane smiled in relief.

"But man, you're as fast as ever, Shirakawa."

"Heh-heh, that's because training is part of my daily routine. Though I'm not as fast as I was during my club days."

It was a surprise to hear that she had been even faster during middle school. Somehow Amane had surrounded himself with people who had outstanding physical and mental capabilities; it made the average Amane feel very jealous.

Kazuya had also attended the same middle school as Yuuta and the others, but since he wasn't a member of the track and field club, he had also been surprised to see her run so quickly.

"I've always wondered this, but how do you move so fast? I guess you don't have much surface area, so that must really reduce the air resistance?"

"Hey, Kazu, what exactly do you mean by 'not much surface area'?"

"Hmm? I'm talking about your height."

Kazuya looked at Chitose with innocent eyes, as if to ask what else he might possibly be referring to, and she frowned back at him.

Her expression was probably not one of anger but of embarrassment. Amane had no doubt she had thought he was talking about her chest.

While Chitose was not as petite as Mahiru, she wasn't exactly tall, either. She was a bit taller than the average girl, but not quite as tall as the other runners. On top of that, she was undeniably slim, so Kazuya must have been surprised by how fast she was.

Amane didn't detect any ulterior motive from the way Kazuya was behaving, so Chitose had just jumped to the wrong conclusion.

"You played yourself on that one, Shirakawa."

"Shut up, Mako."

Chitose's cheeks suddenly flushed red, and she slapped Makoto playfully on the back as she sat down next to him. Amane smirked just a little, so that she wouldn't spot him.

Amane only needed to compete in the ball toss and scavenger hunt, which were both exhibition events, as well as the cavalry battle that all the boys participated in, so he had plenty of time to kill.

Other students who were overflowing with enthusiasm had requested more than two events, but Amane didn't share their zeal. He had only picked two, plus the all-hands match.

The ball toss was already over.

It wasn't an exciting game, just a matter of throwing balls into a basket that was placed up high.

There was usually a scramble to get to the balls to toss into the basket, but there were also usually plenty of balls to go around, so nobody took the event that seriously anyway. It had been a peaceful contest from beginning to end.

It was just a matter of picking up several balls, turning around and piling them up, then tossing them all in, and repeating. A simple task that didn't attract any attention.

But either Amane's aim was more precise, or he'd been more successful at collecting the balls, because he ended up with the most in his basket at the end.

"You really went for the bland events, didn't you, Amane?" Chitose remarked.

"Oh, hush. It's about time for your shift, isn't it? Get going."

"Oh, right. Executive committee members sure are busy..." she grumbled as she looked over her schedule, before heading for the management tent.

Amane wondered why she had volunteered in the first place, but it was too late to say anything.

As Chitose jogged away, Amane checked the agenda for the day, which was posted on one of the tent poles nearby.

The morning program would be over after a few more events. The scavenger hunt, the last event that Amane was participating in as an individual, was one of them.

Once those were finished, everyone would break for lunch before moving on to the afternoon program.

As far as he knew, after his event was over, he would have nothing to do until the cavalry battle in the afternoon.

"...So that means Chitose's in charge during the scavenger hunt, I guess?"

Since she had gone to take her shift just then, that probably meant she would be directing the remaining events. It was a safe bet that she would be judging that one as well... Amane had a feeling Chitose had set it up that way on purpose.

He didn't know who had thought up the scavenger hunt items, but he had a hunch that they were most likely weird and started to feel a little nervous.

Reluctantly, he headed for the assembly spot for the event. When he arrived, Mahiru was already standing there quietly. She had also gotten her choice of events.

He didn't have any particular reason to speak to her, so Amane didn't approach her, but when he made eye contact with her, she smiled faintly and nodded in greeting.

In public, they treated each other as strangers, but Mahiru's real smile revealed itself just a little bit through her placid expression, and Amane's heart jumped in his chest.

He returned the greeting with a blank look on his face, but he couldn't deny feeling somewhat uncomfortable.

As Chitose gathered the participants for the scavenger hunt and finished her duties as a Sports Day administrator, she kept peeking at Amane and Mahiru, looking very pleased.

When it was time for the event to begin, the referee—in this case, that designation belonged to Chitose—entered the grounds.

The field was already scattered with several folded pieces of paper, and when the start signal was given, all the contestants had to do was to pick up one of those slips and go get the things that were written on them.

Unlike the other running events, the scavenger hunt was almost relaxing. The goal was to have fun borrowing the necessary items, so it wasn't that serious of a race.

But depending on the objects, sometimes they were embarrassing to collect, and that was something to watch out for.

"All participants, please take your places at the starting line!"

Chitose smartly issued instructions through a microphone. She made a great master of ceremonies when she wasn't messing around. She had a cheerful personality and could read the mood well. Plus, her voice was easy to hear, clear, and not too high-pitched, which was ideal for making announcements.

Surely she wasn't going to prank them now, Amane thought, not with all the students and staff watching.

"On your marks!" she signaled.

The actual starting pistol was in the hands of another official, a boy—Chitose was just doing the countdown.

"Get set!" Chitose said, then after a pause, the sound of the gun echoed across the field.

No matter how many times he had heard it before, that sound nearly gave Amane a heart attack. Trying not to let it show, he jogged slowly over to the pile of papers.

The faster contestants had already opened up their papers and read what was written on them. Amane followed suit, picking up one of them and checking inside.

Written in meticulous handwriting were the words *Someone you find beautiful.*

Amane had predicted something like this, that they might be sent to retrieve people rather than objects.

He wanted to make a quip about who might have come up with the idea. Fortunately, even Amane would be able to clear this challenge, if only just barely.

He hadn't drawn a paper that said *The person you like,* which would have given him serious trouble. Amane figured he could fulfill the challenge by finding anyone who was objectively attractive.

In other words, someone who anyone would recognize as a beauty... He could call out to Mahiru. Once Mahiru was done collecting her item, they just had to go to the goal together and he could score his points as well.

He was sure to attract a lot of attention being with Mahiru, but he would only be following his instructions. He knew that once everyone heard the item he was supposed to retrieve, they would agree he made the appropriate choice.

With that thought in mind, Amane looked around for Mahiru, who had probably already set off to find her item, when…from beside him, someone grabbed his T-shirt. He felt a tug on his sleeve and turned around to see who it was.

His eyes fell on the person he had just been looking for, staring at him shyly.

"Fujimiya, you are my scavenger hunt item, so when you're finished finding yours, I'd like to ask you to come with me."

"Huh, me?"

"Yes."

He had never imagined they would be each other's object.

In a way, it was convenient, but he had a feeling they were going to draw a lot of attention—but he was already talking with Mahiru in the very center of the athletic field, and they had people already watching them.

On the other side of the finish line, Chitose, the judge, was watching them with a grin.

I'll remember that later.

The words on the scavenger hunt slips were in Chitose's handwriting, so she had probably planted a certain number of them. Amane didn't know what exactly Mahiru had drawn, but since she said she specifically needed him, he was sure she had gotten something nonnegotiable.

"Uhh…what's your item, anyway?" Amane asked.

"It's a secret," she replied. Even though their papers were going to be read aloud after they got to the goal, Mahiru wasn't going to tell him what she was looking for.

So Amane sighed, and they headed toward the finish line.

"You're my item, too, so let's hurry."

"...Then I should ask you, what is your item, Fujimiya?"

"It's a secret."

Mahiru smiled slightly when he answered in the same way.

"I see, then I'm looking forward to finding out after we reach the goal," Mahiru whispered, and took Amane's hand.

Seemingly unbothered by the noise all around them, Mahiru headed for the goal with Amane in tow.

Amane felt a stomachache coming on, but when he saw how cheerful Mahiru was, there was nothing he could do about it—he was but a coward who was madly in love.

A subtle sense that something was amiss washed over Amane as they ran across the field. When they got to the goal, the two of them were greeted by Chitose, who seemed to be in a good mood.

Amane couldn't help but make a face when he saw her, but she didn't seem to pay it any mind.

"What's this, a teaming up?" she marveled. "And here I thought both of you were rivals in this scavenger hunt..."

"Chitose, you jerk, standing over here grinning like a fool. We're both each other's item!"

"Uh-huuuh! All right then, let me confirm your items. Who's first?"

"Start with Fujimiya, please."

Amane was surprised to hear Mahiru single him out, but Chitose seemed to understand why. She gestured to the paper Amane was holding, indicating that he should hand it over.

It wasn't anything that he particularly needed to hide, so Amane readily showed her the item he was looking for.

Chitose made a slightly disappointed face when she saw what was written.

But she pulled herself back together and brought her mouth to the microphone with a smile. "I'm just confirming the item now. The first task for the red team was to find... 'someone you find beautiful'!"

An atmosphere of relief spread through the crowd when the item was read out.

Really, Mahiru had been a safe choice. As far as Amane knew, there was no one in school more beautiful than her—and of course, she was the cutest in his eyes. Setting aside Amane's personal opinion, though, nobody would think twice about his choice.

Amane had felt some animosity directed at him when he'd crossed the goal with Mahiru, but it seemed to have subsided somewhat with the revelation of his object.

The problem lay with Mahiru's item.

Amane didn't know what was written on her slip of paper, but if it somehow specifically indicated him, he couldn't help but feel whatever it was, it wouldn't be good for his quiet student life.

Chitose took Mahiru's paper, blinked several times, then looked at Mahiru again.

Amane couldn't see the words from where he was standing, but he could see the apprehension on Chitose's face. "It's okay for me to say this, right?"

What on earth was the prompt?

After seeing Chitose's reaction, it was even less clear to him now.

Mahiru was still wearing a gentle smile. In other words, she had no problem with Chitose reading it out loud.

After having confirmed again, Chitose donned her usual smug grin.

"Okay, moving right along, they got to the goal at the same time, but anyway, the first task for the white team was to find... 'someone important to you'!"

The moment that Chitose's voice echoed across the grounds, a commotion erupted among the students.

Amane reflexively looked at Mahiru—she was staring right back at him, with her light-pink lips arched upward in a smile.

It was the smile of a child who'd just pulled off some grand prank, with a bit of bashfulness mixed in.

Amane was certain she was peering over to gauge his reaction when he learned what she was looking for.

That cheeky little devil...

Surely it would have been easy for prudent, thoughtful Mahiru to anticipate how their classmates would react to her prompt. Despite that, Mahiru had selected Amane as her object. She'd done it in order to bring about a change in their relationship.

From now on, they could never be strangers again.

She was looking at him with her true smile, the one she showed him at home, not the beautiful, angelic smile that she always had on at school.

Amane grumbled, "We're definitely going to get bombarded with questions after this," and ran his hand roughly through his hair.

"What the hell was that, Fujimiya?"

Sure enough, once the morning events had ended and all the students had returned to their classrooms for lunch, every boy in Amane's class crowded around his desk.

Mahiru, the unattainable girl they all adored, had selected Amane as her "important person" in front of the whole school. Amane understood why they were upset, but being suddenly pressed for answers was still quite vexing.

"Why were you with Shiina?! As her 'important person'?"

"More importantly, since when?"

©Hanekoto

"You were never that close, right?! You just recently started eating lunch together?!"

"What is it?! What is it that she likes about you?!"

"I can't understand it at all!"

Amane faced this rapid barrage of questions with a glassy look in his eyes. Honestly, he had expected some manner of cross-examination, but under the scrutiny of the other boys, he wasn't even going to have time to eat lunch.

The boys weren't the only ones reacting to the news. The girls in his class weren't taking part in the interrogating, but they were shooting him looks, evaluating him, seeming somewhat amused and relieved.

It was probably because Mahiru, the most popular girl in class, now only had eyes for him. Their looks of appraisal were attempts to figure out what kind of person Mahiru had given her heart to.

Amane, who was the focus of attention throughout the classroom, was extremely uncomfortable.

Mahiru herself was absent—she'd gone to buy a sports drink from a vending machine. Itsuki and Yuuta wore troubled smiles as they watched the energetic crowd from a short distance away, and Chitose was enjoying the spectacle with some degree of excitement.

Suppressing the urge to curse his friends for being so insensitive, Amane faced the crowd, doing his best to remain composed in front of his classmates. If he wasn't going to be able to run away anymore, he would have to accept his fate.

Besides, it wasn't like he could disregard Mahiru's feelings. He couldn't ignore the step that Mahiru had taken or the hand that she had extended to him.

He still wasn't especially confident, but even so, he didn't want to dismiss Mahiru's bravery in announcing her feelings publicly. With all that in mind, Amane slowly opened his mouth to speak.

"I can't answer your questions if you shout them all at once," he said, "so at least ask one at a time."

Amane figured that in any case, it would be better to tell the truth from his own mouth than to have people spread rumors willy-nilly, so he steeled his nerves and looked straight at them. The other boys winced.

They hadn't expected Amane to take a proactive stance and open up. It would probably be more accurate to say they hadn't wanted to imagine it.

"...Since when have you been good friends with Shiina?"

"Since last year," Amane answered with as little enthusiasm as possible. He knew that he would have to confess that he was the mystery man who was with Mahiru, a fact which he had previously hidden.

"Huh? Ah, then tell me, the guy we heard rumors about, who was with her at the shrine visit and over Golden Week, was he...?"

"...Me, yeah."

Once he admitted that, it should have been easy for his classmates to make the connection between the "important person" who Mahiru had mentioned before with the "important person" she had just revealed.

Just then, the girl who had apparently seen them on their holiday outing turned to look at Amane, and he looked away uncomfortably.

He felt a little bummed that everyone knew he was the mystery man now, but Mahiru had said that she thought he looked cool, so he was happy enough with that for now.

Amane keenly felt the scrutinizing looks grow more intense as he looked out over the crowd of classmates with the calmest expression he could possibly muster.

"H-how did you become friends?"

"Yeah, you hardly ever interacted! But the real question is why did you pretend to be strangers at first?"

"Well, we live in the same neighborhood, so that's how we know each other," Amane explained. "And the reason why we acted like strangers was because I knew that people would make a fuss just like you're doing now and probably ask a bunch of prying questions."

There was a wave of understanding and sympathetic murmurs from the crowd when he pointed that out. He hadn't said anything because he knew they would react like this. Still, someone must have been unhappy with the idea of their friendship and grumbled, "I don't get it…"

Amane didn't particularly want them to understand, so he let it go.

"…So, Fujimiya, you're dating Shiina?"

One of his classmates asked the question that was probably on everybody's mind.

Amane smiled calmly.

"We are close, and I'm confident that we're each important to the other, but we're not dating. I just wish we were."

He wasn't going to use the word *love*.

After everything that had happened, he only wanted to say that word to the person it was meant for. Truthfully, the scope of his affection for her included many feelings that couldn't all be conveyed by a simple phrase. However, if he wanted to be straightforward, the best way to do it was to say those words to her.

He felt like he was attending his own public execution, but he was at ease knowing there was no need to hide anymore and that he had been able to be outwardly honest.

"But you said that you weren't interested in the angel."

"That wasn't a lie. I have no interest in any angel. Because the one I have eyes for is a girl, named Mahiru Shiina."

The person Amane loved wasn't an angel who was brilliant in both academics and sports, with an attractive face and figure, who was reserved and ladylike and extremely popular. The person he loved more than anyone else was a girl who worked hard, who was lonely because of her bad habit of pushing other people away, who was highly wary, yet extremely vulnerable when she let her guard down— just an ordinary girl, who was wonderful in a completely normal way.

He loved her, not as the angel, but for everything she was inside. To Amane, the heavenly mask that Mahiru wore held no interest at all.

In response to Amane's decisive statement, one of the more assertive boys made an astonished face. With his eyebrows raised, he began to open his mouth to speak.

"Please don't torment him too much, okay?"

The boy froze before he could say anything.

Amane's savior was the other individual at the center of the scandal—Mahiru. She had just returned to the classroom holding a sports drink that was damp with condensation.

When she made eye contact with Amane, Mahiru smiled gently.

"Amane will be troubled if he's not able to eat lunch during the afternoon break."

Mahiru called him by his first name, something only a close friend would do. She clearly had no intention of hiding their relationship any longer.

She showed no signs of being bothered by anyone's gawking— boys and girls alike. Seeming to have run out of patience, the same assertive boy stepped toward her.

The crowd made way for him, sensing that he was going to speak for everybody and ask the questions they all wanted the answers to. Amane's cross-examination was on hold for the moment.

"Shiina! Is Fujimiya your 'important person'?" asked the boy.

"Amane is very important me, yes."

Mahiru had on the same gentle expression as she answered decisively.

The boy flinched for a second when she plastered on her flawless angel smile, but he must have felt the pressure of the crowd behind him, because he continued, albeit a little less forcefully.

"S-so then, um…does that mean that you…like him?"

"Supposing that I do, what would you have to say about it?"

"W-well, it's just…um, if you were going to fall in love…I want to know, why Fujimiya?"

"Why Fujimiya?"

"Ah, well, um, the idea that boring old Fujimiya is dating you, Shiina, it just feels wrong. There are better guys out there!"

"Is that so?"

Amane stared off into space, anticipating trouble. He knew that the boy had inadvertently just set off a land mine.

Mahiru hated it when Amane put himself down. She also said that she hated his unfairly given poor reputation. Which meant that she hated it when other people talked badly about him.

Amane knew that most of his classmates thought he was a very dull person. Unlike when he was with Mahiru, he never really showed his true personality at school. So he thought it was a fair judgment.

But when it came to whether Mahiru would be able to accept that appraisal, that was a different matter.

The look on Mahiru's face did not change. It was the same angelic smile she always wore at school.

But the tension in the air around her was palpable. There was a dangerous glint in her caramel-colored eyes, faint enough that someone close to her would just barely be able to make it out.

"Well, um—"

"And exactly what about him is so boring?"

"Ah, well—"

"Would you please tell me, specifically, what about him is unsatisfactory?"

"Like, his attitude, and his l-l-looks, and—"

"Do you choose who you love based on their face?

"N-no, but—"

"Do you fall in love with people based only on their physical appearance? Will you select your future long-term partner based on how pretty they look?"

As she spoke, Mahiru was still wearing her angelic smile. Despite the friendly expression, Amane could feel tension radiating off of her. He could tell that Mahiru was getting angry.

Amane could feel the irritation even from a distance, so the boy she was staring down probably felt like he was drowning in it.

Indeed, he seemed to have sensed that she was displeased, even as she continued smiling.

Amane could only see the boy's back, but he could tell that his classmate was almost cowering.

"W-well…"

"Actually, in the first place, I don't think you have any right to tell anyone why they can or cannot fall in love with someone else."

The words that came from Mahiru's lips, which were still in a gentle smile, had a sharpness to them that contrasted with her mild tone.

She was still smiling, but she was angry enough that now everyone, not just Amane, could tell.

"I've been a little too harsh, haven't I?" she said. "My apologies."

Mahiru saw that her classmate had become speechless, and she finally eased up a little, giving him an annoyed yet gentle smile. The boy confronting her seemed quite flustered once he realized that he had made Mahiru, who was always mild-mannered and cheerful, quite annoyed.

"I'll take the liberty to correct your statements. Amane is a kind and attractive person. I also think that his quiet, warm presence is simply wonderful. Besides that, he is very gentlemanly, and he always treats me with utmost respect. He's a wonderful person. He supports me when I'm having a hard time and is deeply considerate of my feelings. And at least he never badmouths anyone or tries to get in the way of someone else's romance."

Those words she added at the end were the finishing blow—she had more or less declared that she could never love someone like the boy who had said disparaging things about Amane to her face.

"Is there anything more that you wish to say?"

With a sweet smile, she cocked her head and prompted him for a reply.

The classmate had obviously had enough. He shook his head, and said in a halting and vanishingly small voice, "N-no, there's nothing," then backed away from Mahiru on unsteady feet.

Free from obstructions, Mahiru's gaze landed on Amane.

She had basically announced her love for him in front of all their classmates, and his face stiffened as he wondered how he ought to profess his feelings to her. Mahiru was wearing the best smile he had seen on her yet that day.

It was completely different from her angelic smile—it was the sweet smile full of joy that she showed him at home.

"Let's eat lunch together, Amane."

"…Yeah."

No more boys stepped up to interrogate him.

"…Mahiru really had a lot to say, huh?" Amane mumbled. He had gathered with his classmates to prepare for the cavalry battle, several events after the start of the afternoon program.

"I think it's a shame it had to happen like that," Yuuta said.

Amane furrowed his eyebrows at Yuuta's comment.

The two of them were standing some ways away from the tent because it was annoying to be stared at.

People were still looking his way, but it was at least a little better with some distance.

Yuuta's words implied that Amane should have been the one to make the first move. Amane had no way to refute him.

"I think I get it, but…were Fujimiya and Shiina really that close?" Makoto asked curiously. He seemed a little suspicious of Amane and Mahiru's relationship.

"Mm, honestly, I wondered why they weren't already dating!" Yuuta replied. "If anything, I'm impressed that Shiina was able to hold out this long."

"She really hid it well. Which is understandable, seeing the uproar today at lunch. That was awful, huh?"

Makoto looked at Amane with pity.

Makoto and Kazuya had been in the classroom, but as one might expect, they hadn't been able to speak to Amane while he was being surrounded and questioned. Amane didn't mind, since he wasn't very good friends with them, but he would have appreciated a little help from Itsuki or Yuuta, at least.

"That was really something else. Those guys looked so pathetic, but man, it felt good to watch Shiina shut them all down," Kazuya remarked.

"They looked miserable, but I think maybe from their perspective, it was just too hard to believe…"

"Hmm, you think so? But a guy ought to tell the girl he likes how he feels to her face, right? So it's pretty difficult to pine after somebody when you're not willing to make a move. Just wishing you could have whatever you want without taking any risks, and then whining about it when you don't get your way…it's childish. And then to insult Fujimiya on top of it all? Beyond pathetic."

Amane couldn't help but groan. The idea that a man should confess his feelings affected Amane quite deeply.

"Kazuya, something you said is bothering Fujimiya…"

"Well, from what I can see, Fujimiya was already pretty irritated."

"That's because Shiina expressed her feelings first, you see."

That much was obvious.

Now that things had gone so far, neither Amane nor Mahiru could avoid the truth any longer. There was no question that Mahiru liked Amane.

However, it was clear that the kind of man who sat back without doing anything must have absolutely no self-respect.

Since Mahiru had expressed her feelings directly, Amane knew he would have to respond the same way. He'd known what he wanted to say to her for a long time already; it was just a matter of how to say it.

"I'm planning to tell her properly after we get home. I won't say anything at school."

He felt he should tell her when they were alone, when he could have her all to himself.

Mahiru had already made a public confession, but even so, at least when it came time for them to convey their feelings to each other, Amane was resolved to do it more privately.

Kazuya turned to him with a satisfied-looking smile. "Mm, that's the spirit. But first, we've got some opponents to kick around in the cavalry battle. They're definitely going to come for us!"

For some reason, Kazuya was grinning gleefully, and Amane gave a strained smile back.

Makoto, the one who would be riding on all their shoulders, grumbled wearily, "Don't you think I've got too much responsibility here?" But he sounded more resigned than upset, which was a bit of a relief. "You just follow Kazuya's example, all right, Fujimiya? Really give 'em a good beating."

"I'll handle it."

Amane knew that he was supposed to be fired up and full of manly vigor, ready to fight back any competitors for Mahiru's attention.

I'll tell her everything once we get home.

For that reason and more, Amane hoped he would make it through the afternoon in one piece. The other three boys looked at each other and smiled.

"That was awful…"

After rinsing off what felt like a cloud of dust in the bath, Amane flopped down on the sofa with the feeling of fatigue that always followed vigorous exercise.

Sure enough, the opposing teams had hit them hard during the cavalry battle. But it wasn't a surprise that they would be particularly aggressive toward Amane's team. Still, it had caused a lot of trouble for Yuuta and the others.

But Kazuya had gleefully exclaimed, "Now this is youth!" wearing a warlike grin, so it seemed like he enjoyed that kind of fierce competition.

In the end, Amane's team had not been able to hold out in the face of the white team's terrible attacks, but thanks to the strenuous efforts of Makoto, who had been on top, they had nevertheless managed to snatch many more of the other team's headbands than Amane had expected.

Makoto had been the one doing all the work, but Amane had seen Mahiru, watching from the sideline, smiling at him.

Just like that, the afternoon program ended. Then came the closing ceremony, followed by the customary cleanup after the event.

Now Amane was home.

In a lot of ways, the day had been too much to handle, and Amane was already physically and emotionally exhausted. But it wasn't over just yet.

...I have to tell her.

Mahiru had been brave enough to make her relationship with Amane public; she had chosen to associate herself with him.

He felt like if he failed to respond to her feelings and put off saying anything, he would be a disgrace to all men.

I wonder how I should say it.

Amane had made up his mind, but he was still plagued by hesitation and indecision. It was the first time in his life that he was going to earnestly confess his love for someone, so undoubtedly, he was terrified.

He worried whether the atmosphere was romantic enough for a girl like Mahiru and pondered how he should communicate his feelings so that she would be happy to hear them. No answers seemed to come as the questions swirled around and around in his mind.

Amane pressed his fingers to his forehead, thinking over the possibilities, when—from the front door, he heard a key in the lock.

The sound made him jump because it signaled that the girl occupying his thoughts, who held the spare key to his apartment, was coming to visit.

It was the first time that sound coming from the entryway had set his nerves on edge.

The door closed, and he heard it lock.

Then he heard the echo of slippers walking across the floor, like little breaths of air, and...a familiar girl with flaxen hair appeared in the hallway.

"Amane."

Her light-pink lips were curved gently upward in a tender smile, even sweeter than usual, as though she hadn't been bothered in the slightest by the uproar at school. Amane felt his heartbeat quicken.

Whether she knew how agitated he was or not, Mahiru sat down beside him, as she always did.

There was no more than a hand's breadth of distance between them.

When Mahiru straightened herself up, her hair moved in gentle waves, carrying the sweet smell of her soap. Like Amane, she had taken a bath to wash off all the sweat. If he looked carefully, he could see that her milky white skin was even smoother and cleaner than usual.

Amane's whole body grew tense as Mahiru gave him a refreshing smile.

"Amane, I'm sure you probably have lots of things you want to say to me, and things you want to ask, but...could I ask you to let me say one thing first?"

"S-sure?"

Amane put up his guard, wondering what it could be all of a sudden. Mahiru bowed her head.

"I feel guilty for putting you on the spot and putting you through what I imagine was some very unpleasant attention, Amane. I'm so sorry."

"Huh?"

"...Well, you see," she continued uneasily, "I sort of...knew that would happen."

Amane understood what she had been anxious about. Mahiru knew how influential she was; that was precisely why she was always so careful about the way she presented herself.

So when Mahiru had declared in public that Amane was her "important person," it had been obvious that her announcement would cause a scene, and yet she had done it anyway, knowing the consequences.

"W-well, I more or less already figured that you knew what would happen when you did it, so—"

"You're not angry?"

"I'm not."

"I see, thank goodness."

If anything, as far as Amane was concerned, he'd finally made up his mind precisely because Mahiru had taken the initiative. And now he knew her level of commitment, so he wasn't upset with her at all.

Besides, Amane had also prepared himself to confess his feelings for Mahiru.

He took a deep breath and stared into Mahiru's eyes. They were even clearer and calmer than usual, and gentle enough to make him catch his breath.

"Can I apologize for something, too?" he asked.

"For what?"

"...I'm sorry I've been so cowardly."

Before he could tell her how he felt, there was something else he had to say.

"I'm sorry. I knew how you felt, and I couldn't handle it. I looked away and acted like I didn't notice and pretended like I couldn't see it."

Amane had always vaguely suspected Mahiru had feelings for him, but he had chosen to ignore them. He'd piled up the excuses, telling himself that he was so pathetic that she could never love him as he was, and so on.

But he wasn't going to run anymore.

He needed to confront his feelings and Mahiru's. He wanted to tell her the unvarnished truth.

Amane stared directly at Mahiru, bracing himself so that he wouldn't turn away this time, and—Mahiru smiled a little.

"Well, that goes for both of us, doesn't it?" she said. "I did the same thing... I mean, if I wasn't convinced of how you felt, I never could have taken a step like this."

Mahiru quietly reached out and touched Amane's hand. She was still wearing a faint smile.

"I told you, didn't I?" she said. "I'm a sly one."

"...I don't know. I think I'm slyer."

Amane smiled wryly, thinking that Mahiru's kind of deviousness was awfully cute. Suddenly, he pulled his hand away from Mahiru's grasp and instead wrapped both arms around her and embraced her gently.

He felt her delicate body stiffen with surprise, but then she quickly relaxed in his arms. Mahiru was leaning against his chest and looking up at him. He could see hints of bewilderment and anticipation in her caramel-colored eyes.

"...Will you let me start?" Amane whispered.

Mahiru nodded, her cheeks slightly flushed, and pressed herself further into his embrace.

"Um, so, this is my first time seriously falling for anyone. How can I put this...? I never thought it would happen... I thought it was impossible."

"...Because of your past?"

"Yeah, that's right." He nodded.

He was still embracing Mahiru, not letting her go.

The reluctance that Amane had felt when it came to telling Mahiru that he loved her, or recognizing that she loved him in return, could be blamed on the lasting effects of an incident in middle school.

Amane had no confidence, so he had always been too afraid to express affection toward anyone. When he'd thought about the possibility of being rejected, he had decided it was better not to form any attachments.

That ended after he met Mahiru.

"Because of that, I thought that I wasn't capable of falling in love with anyone… But I never expected someone to change that so easily."

He gazed down again at the girl in his arms. Just looking at her filled his chest with warmth, and he felt like he might overflow with bashful affection.

Mahiru was the first and possibly the last person who would make him feel this way.

That was how in love he was.

"I've realized that people can change when they meet someone they love."

Amane had certainly changed since meeting Mahiru. Thanks to her, he'd finally been able to start breaking free of the wall he had built around his heart and had learned to accept himself bit by bit. The feeling of falling in love with someone had also given rise to the desire to be loved. He had come to know the feeling of wanting to hold someone in his arms and cherish them.

"…You know, at first, I didn't think you had much charm," he admitted.

"I know. You told me to my face."

"I'm sorry about that, really."

Back then, neither of them had thought too highly of the other, and he had said some rude things to her. Mahiru had probably also thought that Amane was an unfriendly, undisciplined loser.

"…You know, when we met, you wouldn't open up to me. You were so distant, but I figured it was okay as long as we got along all right… But before I knew it, that wasn't enough anymore."

When they first met, Amane hadn't wanted to get pointlessly involved with Mahiru. He wondered when that had changed.

"I came to feel like I wanted to learn more about you. I wanted to get to know you. From the bottom of my heart, I wanted to cherish you. I…wanted to be with you. That was the first time I'd ever felt like that."

"…I see."

"I've been holding back this whole time. But…you told me I was enough, so I didn't give up. I tried to think about what I could do to become a better person for you. But, well, before I could do anything, you took the first step."

"Heh-heh…I was holding back too, you know. You're pretty cool, Amane, and I was worried that someone else might come along and snatch you up. I was anxious about whether you'd even like me or not."

"I think you were the only one who was worried about that."

"Hmm. That again…"

Mahiru looked unhappy when Amane put himself down again. But when she noticed his expression, she blinked several times.

Amane wasn't wearing the pitiful face that Mahiru was always so quick to criticize. Instead, his eyes were serious and had the look of someone who had prepared himself to do something especially difficult.

"…So, from now on…I'm going to work hard, so that it's not weird when people see us together."

"Huh?"

"I'm going to become a man who does my best so that no one will tell you that we're mismatched ever again… And even if I can't do it, I still want to improve enough to feel proud of myself."

Amane wanted to become the kind of man who was worthy of standing proudly by Mahiru's side, so that no one could object to their relationship. Not only for Mahiru's sake, but for his own as well. And so that he could have confidence in himself.

The first step down that path had to start with these words.

"I love you, Mahiru, more than anyone else. Will you be my girlfriend?"

He stared into her clear, caramel-colored eyes and whispered his confession. Her serene eyes glistened with tears, but not a single drop spilled down her cheeks. Amane was the only thing reflected in her dewy eyes.

Mahiru closed her eyes and smiled.

"...Yes."

Mahiru's answer was so quiet that even if anybody else had been in the room, Amane would still have been the only one to hear it. Yet her trembling voice conveyed her unmistakable agreement.

Mahiru buried her face in Amane's chest again. Her arms wrapped tightly around his back, holding him firmly in place and not letting go. It was like she was telling him that she wasn't going to let him get away.

Feeling a little embarrassed, Amane also wrapped his arms securely around Mahiru's small back.

—*I'll never let you go.*

I want to treasure you. I want to bring you joy. I want to love you.

Mahiru was the first person to make him feel that way.

"I want to make you happy, Mahiru."

"Is that a promise, Amane?"

Mahiru slowly lifted her face and gave Amane an impish smirk, so he smiled and lowered his lips to her ear.

"This is my wish. So I promise, right now...I will cherish you, and make you happy, absolutely," he pledged passionately.

"...Mm."

Mahiru nodded and gave Amane a sweet smile that melted his heart.

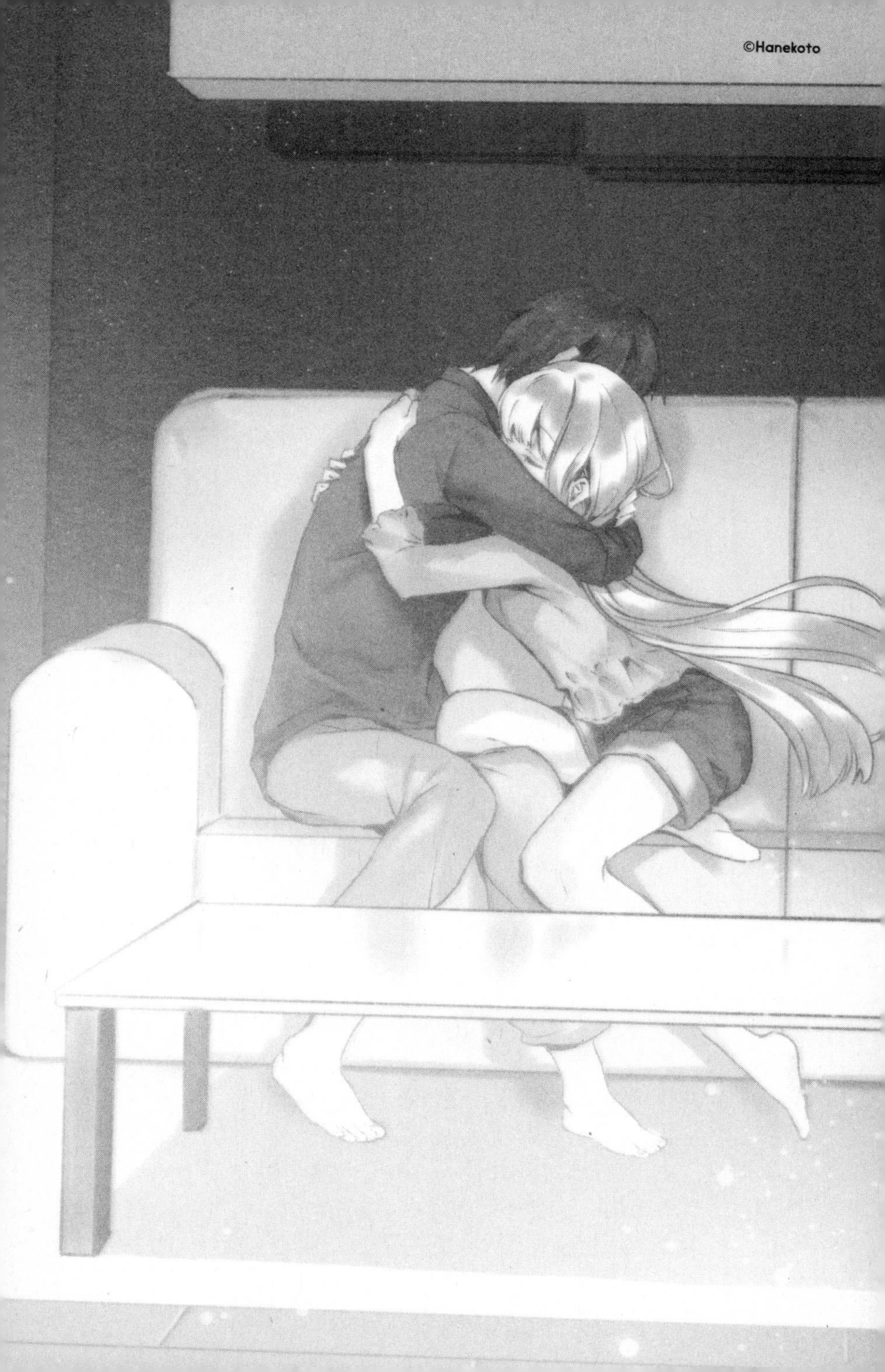

Afterword

It's not over yet, okay?!

With that out of the way, I'd like to thank you for picking up this book. I am the author, Saekisan.

Thank you very much for reading all the way to the end of Volume 4. First, I'd like to say (for the second time) that I have not yet written all that I want to write.

In Volume 4, Mahiru continued to be proactive and really pressured Amane, even as he strengthened his resolve, until they at long last united. Frankly, it was starting to feel weird that they hadn't gotten together yet. It made me realize once again that both of them are really late bloomers.

They certainly took their time getting together, but there's still a long way to go, and from here, I plan to close the distance between them in a painstakingly slow fashion. It's not like Amane's feelings of worthlessness are going to disappear overnight, right? (evil grin)

Starting in Volume 5, the story will focus on what happens after they start dating. I haven't told even half of the story that I plan to tell, so I'm going to continue writing. If possible, I'd like to see an illustration of Mahiru in her wedding dress, and I hope I make it that far!

As always, Hanekoto's fantastic artwork just bursts with emotion. The cover, and the frontispieces, and everything else are all so cute... The domestic feeling and gentle eroticism given off by Mahiru as she ties her hair up are just indescribable. What a luxury, Amane, to have a girl like Mahiru in your house every day!

This time, there were a lot of illustrations with Amane in them, and I'm quite happy about that. The difference in his physique looks good. Amane, the version of you that Hanekoto draws is so cool; how are you still lacking confidence...? Your author is very confused. Isn't Amane so cool?

I think we'll get to see the two lovebirds do some wholesome flirting in the next volume, so I'm looking forward to it.

That's all I have to say, so now I'll thank everyone who helped me along the way.

To the head editor who rendered their services for the publication of this book, to everyone in the editorial department at GA Books, to everyone in the sales department, to the proofreaders, to Hanekoto, to everyone at the printing office—and to all of you who have picked this book up—truly, thank you very much.

I shall lay down my pen here and pray that we can meet again in the next volume.

Thank you for reading to the very end!